TALENT

Juliet Lapidos is a senior editor at *The Atlantic*. Previously she worked at the *Los Angeles Times*, the *New York Times*, and *Slate*. She received her B.A. in Comparative Literature from Yale University and her MPhil in English Literature from Cambridge University, which she attended on a Gates Scholarship.

TALENT

Juliet Lapidos

THE BOROUGH PRESS

The Borough Press an imprint of
HarperCollins*Publishers* Ltd
1 London Bridge Street
London SE1 9GF

www.harpercollins.co.uk

First published by HarperCollins*Publishers* 2019
1

A catalogue record for this book is available from the British Library

HB ISBN: 978-0-00-828120-5

This novel is entirely a work of fiction.
The names, characters and incidents portrayed in it are
the work of the author's imagination. Any resemblance to
actual persons, living or dead, events or localities is
entirely coincidental.

Printed and bound in the UK by CPI Group (UK) Ltd, Croydon CR0 4YY

MIX
Paper from
responsible sources
FSC™ C007454

This book is produced from independently certified FSC™ paper to ensure
responsible forest management.

For more information visit: www.harpercollins.co.uk/green

For Barry, the guardian of my solitude

We see each other in glances.

—FREDERICK LANGLEY

TALENT

Happy Holidays

We met at the supermarket. I was waiting in line to buy the usual nutrient-free snacks—crackers, cookies, Pop-Tarts. She pulled up behind me with a cart full of staples—milk, eggs, canned tomatoes. As we neared the register, she unbuttoned her bright orange trench coat and searched its inside pocket. Whatever she expected to find there was missing. She frisked herself, patting her hips and torso with great urgency until, extreme measures deemed necessary, she removed her coat and shook it upside down. Nothing came out.

"Just my luck," she muttered.

"Everything all right?" I felt obligated to ask.

Smiling apologetically, the woman said she had lost her wallet. Whether she had only herself to blame or a wily pickpocket in the crowded dairy aisle, she couldn't say. Her voice quivered. Her eyes welled with tears. Would I loan her fifty dollars? She'd send me a check that very afternoon. Refusal would have made me seem hard-hearted in the minds of our fellow shoppers who had, I thought, overheard her little performance.

Each morning thereafter I opened my mailbox, anticipating her promised repayment. Each morning thereafter I closed it in a huff. No one wants to feel cheated. I suppose that's why, on a cold winter day roughly two weeks after the incident at the supermarket, I followed my debtor home.

New Harbor felt like a ghost town. The museums were closed. So were the banks on Main Street. Even the Dunkin' Donuts, which was always open, was shuttered. Only the Korean grocery had its lights on. The young woman who sold me a cup of coffee scowled at me when I requested cream and sugar.

I wandered down to the train station and past the large parking lot on Grand Army Avenue. Past the police headquarters, a monstrosity from the brutalist period with no windows at eye level, just yawning ribbed concrete. Past the Elm Street Connector, an abbreviated bit of highway that spat cars from the interstate directly into downtown and in the process bisected the city, a giant gash across its torso.

Rising beyond the connector was the New Harbor Coliseum, a 1970s arena that hosted second-rate hockey teams and outmoded musical acts until around the turn of the millennium, when City Hall announced that it was too expensive to maintain and shut it down. It was a beast and it was empty, a ruin that no tourist would ever visit.

Often caricatured as a pit stop between New York and Boston, New Harbor did have its charms. Like the New Harbor Green, the old town commons of the original Puritan settlement, precisely large enough to accommodate 144,000 souls — the number Revelation says will survive the Second Coming. Or Collegiate's aspirational, neo-Gothic campus, designed to make ignorant Americans think the university dated to the Middle Ages, and visitors from Oxford or Cambridge think, *Haven't I seen this somewhere before?*

Here and there were expensive restaurants, swanky clothing stores with European names, and twelve-dollar-sandwich shops.

Yet there were more vacant lots and vacant storefronts than purveyors of overpriced sandwiches. Beyond the campus orbit, the pleasant spots were like oases in the desert and didn't so much counteract the city's general dinginess as make it more obvious. The fact that New Harbor was formerly considered a quaint New England town also intensified one's awareness of its contemporary squalor. In the 1890s, a very well-known novelist called Hilldale Avenue — a wealthy strip crammed with mansions — "the most beautiful street in America." Or possibly it was a very well-known painter who said that, or possibly the judgment was a local myth. The point being: It was once plausible that a celebrated artist would locate "the most beautiful street in America" in New Harbor. Not anymore. Not unless that artist had a passion for urban decay. The city's gray-brown industrial hues were rarely alleviated by greenery.

In this barren landscape, my debtor stood out. Rather, her trench coat did. She was jogging in place to keep warm at a red light, an orange pogo stick bobbing up and down. The right, the most reasonable, thing was to let the matter drop. Her infraction had been minor, after all, and I had work to do.

I should have gone home, shed my winter layers, and turned on my computer. In twenty minutes or less, a blinking cursor would have replaced the woman from the supermarket as the object of my attention. Instead, I gave pursuit.

She led me farther away from my apartment, farther from the desk where my Word documents waited patiently, and toward Worcester Square. I thought I'd find more activity in that historically Italian neighborhood, but there was no one out to admire the seasonal decorations: the archway draped with colored lights; the crèche in front of an old bakery; the tinsel on benches and bike racks. On St. John Street, the border between Worcester Square and the projects beyond, she paused in front of a gangly white bungalow with a chain-link fence and carpeting on the steps. She went inside and out of sight. I leaned against a cherry tree, wondering if I should ring her bell.

Her name, I learned, was Helen Langley.

For the first time since our initial encounter I observed her closely. In her black flared trousers and striped black-and-white sweater, she looked a bit like a Hollywood Parisian. She wore no makeup and no shoes. Her brown hair, parted down the middle, was white at the roots. Thin wrinkles bracketed her pink lips. Dark blue veins marred her pale skin.

"It's an unusual day to call in a loan," she said, standing at the door, "but whatever. Happy holidays."

"Happy holidays," I replied automatically.

Given the outdoor carpeting, I prepared myself to encounter a correspondingly ugly protective interior, with plastic on the couches and so forth. Instead I found a library-meets-bohemian style: gentle lighting and knockoff-Scandinavian chairs; books all over, on wooden shelving and stacked in every corner, on top of the old television set, on the rug under and around the dining-room table. Helen escorted me through the paper minefield to a den with a picture window facing the street.

"I'll get my checkbook," she said, and she left me alone.

While pursuing Helen I'd felt driven, almost instinctually.

Having gained entry to her house, I felt adrift. I didn't know what I was doing. I didn't know what to expect. I just knew I had a right to be there. In a bid to distract myself, I studied her messy book collection and found a wide aesthetic range: classic works of history, random novels, atlases, almanacs. Although I couldn't discern any order, I saw that the books on the floor were in poor shape, with shabby bindings, whereas the ones piled up by the window seemed freshly restored. I also noticed a jar of glue and sheets of leather.

The radiator hummed. There was a digital clock by the door, the kind that displayed the day and date — 4:01, 4:02.

Holy Mother of God, it was December 25.

That explained it, everything — the closed stores and the Korean girl's frown and the abandoned streets and Helen's greeting. I'd stupidly assumed that she was one of those people who said "happy holidays" generically throughout the season. I should have listened to my mother's voice mail that morning. Amid the nagging and the warning not to procrastinate, she would, I felt certain, have recycled her favorite Jewish-Christmas joke, the one about installing a parking meter on the roof.

I was on the verge of slipping out when Helen came back with a signed check and, adding to my shame, a tray, two cups, two saucers, two spoons, honey, and a pot of hot tea. My perception of my actions had shifted considerably in the past several seconds. What I'd told myself was a perfectly sensible unannounced visit now seemed petty and cruel — I was a regular Scrooge come to darken the holiest day of the year. And whereas I'd thought of Helen as my debtor, my calendrical idiocy meant that I was now more in her debt than she in mine.

Helen settled into an ancient armchair and gestured for me to sit in the one across from her. It sagged under my weight.

"Thank you—for taking me in," I said haltingly, "on Christmas."

She shrugged. "I haven't actively celebrated Christmas since I was a teenager. But I get it. I get the need for company."

"I'm Jewish," I blurted out.

"O. K.," she said, pausing between syllables.

I wasn't certain if she was seeking to reassure or to mollify. The latter seemed condescending. *O.K.* was such a versatile and, therefore, ambiguous word. I pictured it in my head: *O.K. O*, period, *K*, period. Someone sounding out the word for the first time would have pronounced it like Helen did: "*O*" (pause) "*K*" (pause). Modern writers sometimes put periods between words where they didn't belong to communicate dramatic or affected pauses. Got. It. Shut. Up. Screw. You. Up. Yours. But if a writer wanted to convey that a character paused while saying "O.K.," he'd have to do so explicitly because of that word's peculiarities. It calmed me to think of orthography instead of the fact that Helen was looking at me intently, waiting for me to speak. Her irises were bright green. Her eyelids drooped close to the nose. Her spirit animal was the gecko.

"Holiday decorations go up earlier and earlier every year!" I said.

"They don't, though. Thanksgiving week. Always."

"I'm pretty sure—"

"Always."

I stirred my tea, silently conceding the point.

"All the stuff in here, what is it?" I asked, trying a different tack. "The leather and the glue?"

"It's my work. I'm an antiquarian and a bookbinder."

"That sounds interesting."

"Does it? I have to think about old books all day."

"So do I. I study English."

Helen scrunched her nose, either because she didn't like English or because her tea was too bitter.

"At Collegiate, I guess."

Usual reactions included feigned indifference ("Nice place, I hear"), eager networking ("Do you know..."), harsh one-upmanship ("Princeton said no?"), and classist disdain ("State school was good enough for my kids").

"I'm not surprised. You have that look," she said, indifferently disdainful. "Anyway, your relationship with old books is not like mine. Academics care about the ideas inside a book. Antiquarians care about dustcovers and bindings."

"Don't the contents matter at all?"

"Reputation matters. Famous books cost more than forgotten ones. Basically, though, we're materialists, or fetishists." Helen grinned as if she'd said something adorably naughty. "Our clients are fetishists too. They don't buy books they want to read. They buy books they consider physically special because they're rare or unusual: first printings, books signed by the author, books once owned by a notable politician. If they really cared about the contents, they'd just find a used two-dollar paperback."

Helen's delivery was fluid and monotone, almost as if she'd given her speech many times before. Perhaps she had. Perhaps she often had to explain how antiquarians were different from scholars. I was struck by her dismissive characterization of her chosen profession and by the pleasure she took in making it seem unintellectual. She was proud of her fetishistic materialism in the way a certain sort of American was proud of never having traveled to a foreign country.

"Maybe you know my uncle," she said.

"Is he in the English department?"

"In a manner of speaking. He was a writer. Freddy Langley. Frederick, in print."

I would never have guessed. Langley was a common name and Helen seemed, to me, unartistic: the sloppy scene at the supermarket, the orange trench coat, her line of work. *This* woman? *That* man?

Once the initial shock passed, I felt titillated by the connection, even a little flushed, and then, immediately, ashamed by my reaction. I looked down on people who texted their friends if they happened to sit next to a celebrity at a restaurant. Yet I felt something like self-importance because I was sitting across from the niece of a well-known author. Physical proximity to genetic proximity to fame.

After sunset we were left with only the light from a standing lamp. In the dimness, the den felt cozily antique. And I felt fine. I'd moved from anxiety to acceptance and now something resembling enjoyment in the strangeness of the situation. One day it would make a good story: The evening I drank tea with Frederick Langley's niece. On December 25.

"I should tell you something," I said, blushing. "I didn't realize, when I rang your doorbell, that it was Christmas."

Helen laughed. She looked away from me and out the window. It was too dark to discern the street or the neighboring houses. Still, I aped her. If someone had walked by he might have noticed two women staring straight in his direction, into the night, one face past life's midpoint, the other past youth, in a cluttered room protected from the winter cold. We would have made for a nice painting, a portrait of what I supposed, in my ignorance, was the last time we would ever see each other.

Other People's Perspiration

There were no Pop-Tarts left in my kitchen cabinet, presenting me with a choice: Skip breakfast or get dressed and walk to the store. Theoretically, there were other options available to me. I could, for instance, have resorted to the organic steel-cut oatmeal that I'd purchased in a fit of attempted self-improvement. But I'd gone too far by selecting the non-instant variety, and the thought of struggling at the stovetop was grossly unappealing — particularly since my reward for that labor would be . . . oats. Organic oats.

On the one hand, it was cold out. On the other hand, I was hungry. I stood in my kitchen, paralyzed by the prospect of making a decision. Again I rifled through the cabinet, hoping for a different result. Winston Churchill said a fanatic is someone who can't change his mind and won't change the subject. Maybe I'd get lucky. Maybe I'd surprise an old box of Pop-Tarts hiding behind worthier items.

My meeting with my doctoral adviser was at four p.m., in four hours. Factoring in time to shower, dress, and walk to the English department, I had three hours and fifteen minutes to prepare. It was time to move on from the Pop-Tarts problem. It was time to act decisively. Was it possible, though, to work well on an empty stomach?

Innumerable listicles suggested otherwise. The kitchen smelled like chemical lemon zest, the cleaning company's signature scent. The stone tile felt chilly on my bare feet. I could skip breakfast or get dressed and walk to the store. Either way, I would eventually have to get dressed. Moreover, I would eventually have to shower. Or would I? Perhaps showering wasn't strictly necessary. On second thought, it was not. Getting dressed, however, obviously was.

I matched a pair of jeans from my hamper with thick socks from a pile of clothes and old running shoes from the depths of my closet. And then I wrapped myself in a winter cocoon. And then I paused at the door, feeling cold air seep from the hallway into my apartment. And then I slipped off my running shoes and removed my hat. And then I put both articles back on and launched myself past the threshold.

One spends much of one's life saying, or thinking, *And then*. And then I'll graduate. And then I'll get a job. And then I'll get married. And then I'll have a kid. And then the kid will go to school. And then I'll get divorced. And then the kid will get married, and then divorced.

Or just: And then I'll review my notes. And then I'll see my adviser. And then I'll go home. And then I'll order dinner. And then I'll watch television. And then I'll fall asleep.

Seeing as I was no longer a teenager, I limited myself to unfrosted Pop-Tarts at breakfast. These came in five different flavors: strawberry, brown-sugar cinnamon, wild berry, apple, and blueberry. The middle three were revolting. The first and last were equally good. By 12:45 I had one strawberry and one blueberry spooning in my toaster. By 12:50 I was sitting on the rolling chair at the desk in my bedroom, ready to work on my dissertation, resisting the siren song of my down comforter. The desk was a mahogany behemoth out of place in our digital age, with its stacked drawers, shelves, and nooks meant to hold the debris of an intensely physical time. The down comforter was fluffy and soft. I rolled over to the bed. I rolled back to the desk.

The former owner of the desk, deceased, had, in his lifetime, been a usurer in charge of a veritable army of usurers, or so my mother had told me — I'd hardly known him, my grandfather. He was a highly successful, disreputable businessman who, from what I gathered, had clawed his way out of poverty by sinking other people into it. This was abhorrent. However: He'd left me the desk and a heap of money, so I was inclined to forgive his tactics and think kindly of him. Without his largesse, I would have led a far less pleasant life. I might have had to earn petty cash by grading moronic undergraduate papers, leaving me little time for research, including the research currently spread out on my grandfather's desk.

The nutritional facts on the back of the Pop-Tarts box informed me that a strawberry pastry contained two hundred calories, fifty of which came from fat. The first ingredient was enriched flour, the ninth was dried strawberries, followed by dried pears, dried apples, and leavening. A blueberry pastry was identical in every way except that it contained dried blueberries rather than dried strawberries.

My dissertation, my heartbreaking work of staggering scholarship, was very nearly finished. Soon I would print out the two-hundred-plus pages for the last time. Soon I would bring those pages to the university copy shop and have them bound in leather. Soon I would enter the job market and bask in the praise of the usually taciturn interviewers, uncorked by my greatness. Next I would turn my dissertation into my first book. I would receive grants. I would accept visiting professorships in Paris and Rome. I would give well-attended talks at literary festivals. My scholarship would breach the academic-real-world divide and grace the pages of the *New York Review of Books*. A dark-haired man with a British accent would recognize my virtuosity and excuse my lack of charm.

Any student of narrative would agree that my life had been leading up to a brilliant dissertation and a secure position at a top-notch university. Of course that was my future; it was a matter of course. Even as a child, when my mother read to me at night, I knew where the stories were headed and could guess the characters' motivations. *That's the protagonist's long-lost sister, I'm sure of it. The man in the mustache will betray his betrothed for her diamond earrings. Why else would the author linger on their shiny contours?* I had never seriously considered a career unmoored to reading and writing.

Narratively speaking, success could not but lie ahead for the valedictorian of a pressure-cooker high school who had finished summa cum laude at an elite college and had her pick of graduate programs. As had been expected, Bs an affront to her — my — honor. At twenty-two, I published my first article. (A spruced-up version of a term paper on the use of coincidence in Paul Auster's *Moon Palace*.) At twenty-four, I published a second. (Mistaken identity as allegory for literary misinterpretation in Henry Fielding's *Tom Jones*.) At twenty-six, I passed my oral exams with high honors. There was just one step left for me to take, a step that would come as naturally as — as taking steps. As walking.

Titled "Where Does Art Come From?" my dissertation was an

intellectual history of inspiration. To early civilizations, it was a gift—or curse—from the gods. The ancient Greeks held the Muses responsible for inspiration, which they distinguished from skill or technical ability; mere artisans toiled to refine their craft, whereas artists were mouthpieces for what divine entities wished to express. But if ventriloquism was semiautomatic, it was still exhausting and not exactly fun. Plato in *Ion* described poetic inspiration as a sort of possession, a maddening ordeal.

The Hebrew tribes also looked to the divine. Samuel gave Saul fair warning that Yahweh's inspirational methods were heavy-handed: "The spirit of the Lord will come powerfully upon you, and you will prophesy . . . and you will be changed into a different person." Christians replaced Yahweh with the Holy Ghost. Tertullian, for instance, explained that God, through the Holy Ghost, "flooded" the minds of the prophets. Granted, Jews and Christians were preoccupied with revelation, not epic poetry, but in those days there wasn't such a clear distinction between theology and fiction.

As Western societies became more secular, the explicit God talk fell out of fashion. The Romantics compared the artistic process to a passive chemical reaction. They argued that poets were—unconsciously—sensitive to mysterious energies or winds, which they converted into creative enterprise. Yes, wind was a metaphor, but not for anything terribly concrete. "Poetry," Shelley said, "is not like reasoning, a power to be exerted according to the determination of the will." On the contrary, "the mind in creation is as a fading coal which some invisible influence, like an inconstant wind, awakens to transitory brightness."

Then along came Sigmund Freud, who said that what his forebears had thought was supernatural or, at any rate, external to the self was actually the subconscious at work. Writers wrote, painters painted because of early childhood trauma, deep psychological wounds, which they sublimated into poems, novels, paintings. Marxists, for their part, thought that was just as silly as Shelley's fading-coal theory. They looked not to infancy but to the economy, theorizing that art was always, necessarily, an expression of social conditions. Artists were mirrors.

Although the concept of inspiration had changed dramatically over the centuries, I argued that one element remained steady: Everyone seemed to think that it was out of the artist's control. The artist cannot train the Muses or the Holy Ghost. He cannot force his mind to channel inconstant winds. He cannot will his parents to traumatize him. He cannot tame macroeconomic trends.

I also argued that, although this lack of control in one sense minimized the role of the artist, it simultaneously made the artist seem special. Art was not just another trade. If a young woman decides she wants to be a doctor, she can go to medical school and learn about the human body. If a young man decides he wants to be a builder, he can find a job at a construction company and learn about concrete. But if that same young woman or young man decides, *No, I'd rather be an artist,* then it's game over. You're out of luck. Unless, that is, you happen to have been chosen by God/have the right disposition to channel winds/have had a difficult childhood. Either you've been touched, or you haven't.

But—this was totally ridiculous, was it not? All sorts of people from all sorts of backgrounds became artists, and no brain scan had ever discovered some artist-specific pathway. Each and every theory of inspiration was bullshit designed to make artists feel as though they belonged to a special class, even though there was no evidence of that class beyond the tautology that all artists had something in common — which was that they were artists.

"It's a little thin," said Professor Carl Davidoff. My adviser was short and pudgy and somehow pulled off the trick of looking swarthy despite having light skin, a result of his thick, dark, almost black curly hair and equally thick, dark eyebrows. For a full professor, he was young, in his late thirties. He cleaned his glasses to avoid taking in my expression. "The historical overview is fine but your conclusion, your actual thesis, feels a little thin," he repeated.

"Care to elaborate?"

"My assessment is more or less the same as it was three months ago, and six months ago, and twelve months ago. It doesn't seem to be sinking in —"

"This has changed *a lot* in the last twelve months —"

"Let me finish, Anna," he interrupted. He was in the habit of using my name when he wanted to convey that he meant business, like a kindergarten teacher scolding an unruly five-year-old. "It's a good observation: There's a seemingly universal tendency to place inspiration beyond the artist's control. You believe this tendency, this assumption, is wrong, even stupid. Fine. But if you really think that all theories of inspiration are stupid — *all* of them — then you need to suggest an alternative. I've said this before. You keep ignoring me and fine-tuning what you have instead."

"It's just work."

"What is?"

"That's my alternative theory. There's no such thing as inspiration. Writing is work like anything else. It's just creative work instead of physical work or what have you. Bankers bank. Plumbers plumb. Sculptors sculpt. Writers write. I once heard Naomi Wolf quote her father: 'The writer who goes out with the bucket daily seems to provoke the rain.' He had the guts to make art sound mundane."

"Citing other people's arguments won't impress me. You always do that when you're not sure what to say. If you believe the Wolf line, do the work of proving it. You need a case study. I've said this before: Enough with the lit review. Choose an author to examine closely. His biography. His output. Think about what it is that caused him to write. Connect what happened off the page to what happened on it. Don't smirk. This is basic. Fisher-Price My First Academic Paper."

"Wow."

"Sorry. I'd recommend Milton if there weren't already dozens of books on his process. He spent years after university obsessively reading the classics without writing much at all, living off his father's investments. He traveled through Europe, still not writing, dabbled in politics, then, finally, drafted a drama that would become his epic. He said it came easily! You must know the line— the celestial patroness who nightly dictates to the slumbering poet his 'unpremeditated verse.' "

"How nice, to wake up and find a few more pages of *Paradise Lost* at your feet."

Better than a nocturnal emission, I did not add.

Professor Davidoff's office, laid out like a psychoanalyst's with a leather armchair for him and a leather couch for his visitors, was overheated and stuffy. I wondered why he didn't open the window since he was visibly uncomfortable; a few beads of sweat had trickled down his forehead and I had to resist the urge to dab him with a tissue. Some future civilization would master temperature control.

It was thirty degrees outside and what felt like eighty degrees inside, hastening climate change.

"I should ask—is there something going on?" he said.

"No."

"Some reason you're finding it so hard to finish?"

"My parents think I'm lazy."

"Oh?"

"They say I need to stop procrastinating."

Professor Davidoff scratched the dry skin around his nose, a compulsive habit.

Again the conversation flagged and I thought back to the time, many years earlier, when I'd attended a Quaker meeting in backwoods Vermont. It began with twenty minutes of enforced silence, at the end of which congregants were encouraged to speak their minds if "the Spirit moved" them. It didn't move anyone. Three-quarters of an hour in I felt so oppressed that I considered jumping up, maybe reciting poetry. But I only knew Ogden Nash by heart, which didn't seem appropriate.

> *Anxious parent, I guess you have just never been around;*
> *I guess you just don't know who are the happiest people*
> > *Anywhere to be found;*
> *So you are worried, are you, because your child is turning*
> > *Out to be phlegmatic?*

The professor lurched inelegantly out of his chair, walked cautiously, like a much older man, over to his desk, and shuffled his papers. His suit jacket had deep creases along the shoulder blades, suggesting he didn't have someone at home to look him over. He did, though: a viperous woman who always served me last at end-of-year dinner parties, certainly because her husband had predicted, at the first of these parties, that I would one day sit alongside him as a colleague. She was jealous of what our relationship was, or had been; a relationship between a man who was fiercely proud of having graduated from Williams, Cambridge, and Princeton — he'd framed his diplomas and mounted them to the wall above his desk — a man who looked up to no one, straight ahead to almost no one, and a young woman with the potential to match him. If she'd heard his Fisher-Price quip, she might have treated me rather differently.

"No . . . no . . . no," the professor muttered, to himself as much as to me. "Here it . . . no. Now, where did I put that? Hang on. Yes, this is it."

He unfolded a week-old university newsletter and pointed to an item on the second page that read *Francis Goodman, the* New York Times *bestselling author and life-hacking expert, will deliver a lecture on efficiency and work-flow techniques at the School of Management on January 15.*

That was it. The professor squinted at me.

"You might find it useful," he said.

"You're joking."

"Not at all."

"The dissertation's close. I think it's close. It's close, isn't it?"

"I'll be frank, Anna."

On weeknights, GPSCY, the offensive-sounding Graduate and Professional Student Center on York, sold two-for-one margaritas. After my meeting with Professor Davidoff I ventured there, as I'd learned from movies that in moments of distress, adults invariably resorted to alcohol. The bartender looked me over brazenly to see if I was worthy of his unwanted attention and apparently decided that I was not.

Another failed romance. Aborted. Uprooted. For months that side of my life had been totally dormant; my last flirtation had ended disastrously. Benjamin was a student at the medical school who said he wanted to help people but would probably end up a plastic surgeon. For our fifth date he'd invited me to the movies and, to seem worldly, had picked out a French film called *Baise-moi*, which he thought meant "kiss me." It meant "fuck me" and had been banned in several countries because it featured numerous graphic rape scenes. Our fragile relationship couldn't handle the awkwardness.

Double-fisting margaritas, I drifted through the bar, eventually spotting someone I knew in one of the red-pleather booths: Evan. He was my contemporary in the English department and a notorious grind, the kind of guy who never turned in anything late, never left the library before it closed, never went on vacation without his laptop. He'd once considered me a rival.

I liked to think, though, that my mild distaste for his company came not from competitive anxiety but from a tribal aversion to his ethnic whiteness. He was a high WASP with perfectly coiffed blond hair, prominent cheekbones, a square jaw, broad shoulders, and a seemingly endless supply of Nantucket Reds. That night he wore a Barbour jacket, which added to the impression that he might start shooting foxes at any moment.

Out with Evan was another classmate, Evelyn, who also played the role of Evan's fiancée. She had smooth black hair (inherited from her father, a Chinese ophthalmologist) and symmetrical features (inherited from her mother, an Alabama hand model). Her most notable trait was dullness: she never said anything particularly smart, funny, or controversial. Mostly she echoed and amplified Evan. Under his influence, she'd even embraced a Northeastern prep-school aesthetic, filling her closet with pastel slacks and cashmere sweaters.

When she saw me she waved like a beauty queen on a float, beckoning me to approach. She said they'd descended on GPSCY to celebrate Evan, whose job search was going well. The University of Chicago wanted to fly him out for an interview.

"Congratulations!" I managed.

"Thank you. Are you here by yourself?" Evan asked, noticing that both my hands were full.

"Tequila's good company."

Evan peered vacantly into the middle distance while Evelyn bragged on his behalf: More than five hundred people had applied for the tenure-track position at Chicago, many of them already assistant professors at other universities. Only five of them had been offered interviews, and Evan had cause to believe that he was the front-runner. On the phone, the head of the hiring committee had said that he was "very, really, very impressed" with Evan's "precocious and lively" dissertation on moments of enlightenment in mid-twentieth-century American literature. When he heard that Evan was in a committed relationship with another graduate student — meaning Evelyn — he said Chicago might be able to find her an adjunct position. It didn't even cross Evelyn's mind to feel ashamed of a hanger-on posting. For Evelyn, engagement meant parasitic self-abnegation. She would henceforth derive her value entirely from her partner's success.

"Nothing's certain yet," said Evan, "but I have a good feeling."

"So do I," said his amplifier. "I'll keep my fingers crossed, for both of us."

Like a film critic for a small-town rag, Evelyn resorted routinely to set phrases. She'd — famously — once described *Romeo and Juliet* as "a refreshingly good love story." In response, Professor Davidoff had called her an "evolutionary cul-de-sac" — the best insult that I had ever heard.

Evan and Evelyn were happy in Evan's success. Oh so happy.

"I wonder — just thinking out loud here — if Chicago is a safe place to live?"

"What? What are you talking about?" asked Evan.

"Lots of gangs there, so say the newspapers. High murder rate. Muggings. Drive-by shootings. You'll need to watch yourself if this works out."

Evelyn glared at me. She was as toothlessly protective as one of those tiny dogs that travel in purses.

"Chicago's dangerous, sure. That's why the university has one of the largest private security forces in the country, right up there with the Nation of Islam," Evan said, determined to put down my rebellion swiftly. "I think they can shield me from spraying bullets while I teach. Anyway, who cares what the city's like so long as the university in that city has a good reputation? That's what matters for my career."

Appropriately, the conversation turned to "our work," and I

tried hard to enter a meditative state in which the mind separates from the body, no longer registering external stimuli. I must have succeeded because the next thing I knew, Evan was saying: "Everything all right?"

"Sorry, what?"

Evelyn took the liberty of answering: "He said, how about you? What are you working on?"

I'll be frank, Anna: You've fallen behind. Find a case study. A good one. Do it right away.

Instead of prevaricating, I changed the subject, offering to pay for a round of shots. My classmates struggled to remember the proper order of operations. Lime, then salt, then liquor? Liquor, then lime, then salt? Not that it really mattered. Unlike baking a cake or solving a math problem, the sequence didn't affect the result: drunkenness. Evelyn coughed, sending flecks of spit in my direction. I thought of her cozy in Chicago's Hyde Park, an adjunct professor, a professor's wife, and my stomach constricted, as if the day's disappointments were crawling through my gastrointestinal tract. On consideration, that may have been the tequila.

The restroom — I'd never before had reason to appreciate — was intended for individual use, meaning I wouldn't have to worry about eavesdroppers in adjacent stalls. My stomach constricted again as I touched the door handle, sticky with other people's perspiration. A good alliterative title: Other People's Perspiration. I removed my sweater and found a relatively un-ghastly place for it on the floor. If I had to buy a new one, so be it. Still too hot, I removed my T-shirt and then crumpled. It seemed like a fantastic idea to press my face against the porcelain toilet, the stand part that connects to the floor. I could see streaks of urine along the sides but

I didn't care. The coolness of the porcelain was more important, as refreshing as a good love story.

Toilets were amazing devices. Their beauty was, of course, universally recognized, at least since Marcel Duchamp, but enough could not be said about their practical worth. As an engine for flushing waste, toilets were arguably more important for civilization than more vaunted engines: the steam and internal combustion. They used only gravity and water. Just gravity, water, and ingenious design to keep away infection and keep at bay the rough truth of our disgusting animality.

Pre-toilet, even aristocrats had to live with their waste nearby until servants came around to remove their chamber pots. They stowed their shit and piss beneath their beds and slept on top of it. The smell during asparagus season must have been nightmarish. Whereas I, a lowly graduate student who'd fallen behind, could make my vomit disappear by applying pressure to a trip lever.

The Notebook

Alana catches the train from Boston to Cincinnati, snagging a window seat. Deborah sits next to her and strikes up a conversation about fur coats. It's as good a topic as any. War. Peace. Life. Death. Fur coats. When Deborah exits the train, Eleanor takes her place. Eleanor's topic is animal cruelty. After Eleanor, Francine talks pet insurance, and Georgina talks vegetarianism. Alana politely plays her part, never acknowledging the alphabetical chain or thematic connections, which, anyway, never amount to anything. Not only is there no climax, there is no sense of building, of anything wagered or gained. Each conversation, each story, is as meaningless and effervescent as the last. If there's any point at all it's to show my hand.

Sergeant Davis calls his troops together. Vietnam. They need a volunteer for a perilous mission. "I'll do it, sir," says Private Johnny Johnson. Sergeant Davis describes what Private Johnson has to do in extreme detail, every step of the way, to retrieve medical supplies accidentally dropped behind enemy lines. This will go on for pages

and pages until the reader feels bored stiff and
absolutely despises me. Private Johnson salutes his
superior in a patriotic fervor. He sets out. Before he
can complete step one he trips over a branch right onto
a mine and gets blown up. Guts everywhere.

Strange to say Vietnam was nothing to me. Five years
younger, it would have been everything. I was just old
enough not to have to really care, in life or in writing.
A lucky year for boys, 1938. What would the Chinese
call it? Year of the . . . some animal just the right size
to hide in a burrow while the predators get their fill.

Lewis and Don, old school friends, haven't seen each
other in years and years, stretching into decades. Too
long. Far. Too. Long. Lewis recently won a prize—he's
an architect—and he can't wait to tell Don all about it.
Before Lewis gets the chance, Don starts talking about
himself. He got a raise at work. His mistress is young
and beautiful. His car is fast. His son is a quarterback.
Banal, small-bore stuff, not nearly as significant as
the prize. (The prize is a Big Deal.) Lewis is turned
off. He decides not to share his accomplishment. And
suddenly he feels wonderful. Elated. He doesn't
understand but what's happened is simple enough.
What he doesn't share belongs to him alone.

I was fourteen, skipping rocks at Walden Pond.
Veronica Lancet was there with her family but she

managed to get away from them. In a quiet moment she kissed me. It was my first kiss. I remember her tongue felt like wet fruit. I remember, when I looked at her the next day, feeling like an ice cube coming apart in hot tea. Extremities tingling. Heartburn-like sensation around the, um, heart.

Freddy Remembered

The promotional brochure that Collegiate sent to newly admitted students had a picture of Golden Memorial Library on the cover. Golden was meant to resemble a Gothic cathedral, which it more or less did. Construction crews must have exhausted New England's quarries to assemble its granite and limestone façade; must have wondered if they were, in fact, building some sort of church when they erected the portentous entrance hall, with its sixty-foot vaulted ceiling, and the fifteen-story tower destined to hold books — millions upon millions of books acquired as part of a literary arms race with the nation's competing research universities.

Below Golden was New Campus, an underground library that Collegiate never featured in its advertising materials. Whereas Golden was lousy with stained glass and gargoyles and marble reliefs and chandeliers, New Campus had buzzy fluorescent lights, cubicles shaped like swastikas — if you took the bird's-eye view — white plaster walls, and poster reproductions of forgotten midcentury pop art. Golden had overstuffed couches and internal courtyards. New Campus had "weenie bins": windowless, closet-size rooms for private study. To move from Golden, built in the 1920s, to New Campus, built in the 1970s, was to witness the devolution of American architecture.

Yet there was something comforting about New Campus. I was sitting in a swastika, hungover, determined to thicken my too-thin dissertation, and as I stared at an ancient water spot, I reflected that New Campus did not demand anything of its visitors, like Golden did. Golden expected heady gratitude. New Campus accepted wallowing.

A PhD in English should, in theory, take five years. In reality, it was considered well within the range of normal to finish in seven. But I was midway through that seventh year and still the end evaded me. Relatives who'd once admired my precocity were beginning to wonder what was taking so long. "What, still in school?" my aunts and uncles asked at family gatherings, doubtful they'd heard me right. I was twenty-six, then twenty-seven, then, to my amazement, twenty-nine. A terrible, liminal age. As if by sleight of hand, my twenties had disappeared. They'd oozed into books I couldn't remember reading, seminars I couldn't remember attending, conversations I couldn't remember having.

I'll be frank, Anna: You've fallen behind. Find a case study. A good one. Do it right away.

The muscles under my right shoulder blade were throbbing again, the rhomboids. I slouched along them — I sat lopsided, right lower than left — and they protested this treatment frequently, sending bursts of pain diagonally across my back. The problem wasn't bad enough to drive me to a doctor, but it should have been sufficient to make me improve my posture. Should have; was not. It helped to stretch both arms above my head and thrust my chest forward. Arms up; chest out.

Six and a half years in New Harbor. Three years since I'd passed my oral exams; three summers, with the length of three long winters. Roughly 1,100 days; 26,400 hours; 3,000 meals; 300 Pop-Tarts; 120,376,000 heartbeats — my Nokia had a calculator —

assuming an average resting rate of seventy beats per minute. And in that span of time: *It's a little thin.*

That judgment applied equally well to my social life. Other people could excuse their lack of progress by pointing to offspring or a passionate affair or even an obsessive interest in something pleasurable but meaningless, like video games or football. I could not account for what I did all day. I walked around. I read. I ate. Sometimes I loitered in pharmacies, overwhelmed by branded bounty. What else? Next to nothing. I had nothing to distract me from nothing.

My rhomboids whined as I considered the possibility that I would have to find a new career, start afresh in some horribly grinding profession like the law, the last refuge of the academic. How awful it seemed to go back to the beginning. How tiring to study for the LSAT and ask my disappointed parents to pay for law school or dig into my inheritance to do the same and then have to actually attend law school and, worse yet, have to actually practice law. No. No. I wasn't there yet. No. I was O.K. *O*, period, *K*, period. I knew what I was doing. I was a star — or had been recently and could be one again. Would be one again. Just as soon as I found a case study. A good case study. Which I would do right away. Of course I would.

The water spot on the ceiling looked like a rabbit with fangs. One ear turned down, the other upright, drops of blood trickling from long teeth. There was a word for this psychological phenomenon, seeing images of animals or faces in clouds or on the surface of the moon or in stains. But I couldn't remember it. There was also a word for the inability to remember a word, which I couldn't remember either, although I knew it sounded Greek — contained

Greek—and that the Swiss psychiatrist Carl Jung had coined it. Amnelogia, maybe. I could, at least, recall the various words that meant "behind": *delinquent, overdue, delayed, belated,* and *retarded,* the last of which was sadly unacceptable, no matter the context, thanks to the euphemism treadmill.

My laptop had gone to sleep. A flick of the touchpad revealed my dissertation. Forget it. I slinked over to the Fiction and Literature section, found the twentieth century, and pulled out a copy of *Frederick Langley's Complete Works.*

I first heard the name Frederick Langley in middle school when my eighth-grade English teacher recommended *Brutality and Delicacy.* He impressed upon me that Langley was a serious author and made clear he wouldn't entrust just anyone with Langley's work. It was a mark of distinction. Although reading Langley felt like my official introduction to literary culture, the aura of formality in no way spoiled my pleasure. I encountered Langley slightly before it became automatic for me to underline or take notes, that prelapsarian period when fiction was just for enjoyment.

My attachment was short-lived. In high school, I became acutely aware that the students who didn't care for reading cared for Langley the most. They found him delightfully outrageous. They loved "Longer," the grotesquerie in which the circumcised protagonist tries to regrow his foreskin. One boy could recite the entire dinner-table scene from memory. His girlfriend pledged never again to eat calamari.

The idiots liked Langley. The idiots who thought they were countercultural because they were bad at tests. The idiots who thought that any book published before the twentieth century was boring. The idiots owned that dumb T-shirt with a bulging eyeball on the front and, on the back, *We see each other in glances*. The idiots never bothered to learn the difference between a dactyl and an anapest—didn't see the point—yet had the energy to track down old magazine articles about the time Langley wowed a Greenwich Village crowd: he'd read the first half of a story and then improvised three possible endings. (And it really did require energy to find those articles. I went to high school in the dark pre-Google age, when the internet was still the domain of math nerds and pedophiles, so the idiots' best option was microfiche.)

The idiots liked Langley. So I stopped liking Langley. The fact that Langley was my introduction to literary culture made him seem introductory. The fact that I enjoyed reading his stories made them seem frivolous. I formed the impression that he wasn't sophisticated. He was, in my adolescent assessment, serious enough for a serious eighth-grader, not for a budding literary critic. That judgment stayed with me. Still, when Helen told me that she was Frederick Langley's niece, the information produced in me a childish excitement.

I skimmed the introduction to *Complete Works*, which divided Langley's stories into two major categories, "epiphanies" and "compulsions." The epiphanies were formulaic: something happens to X that changes his perspective on Y.

The quintessential epiphany was "Alone at Green Beach," featuring an eleven-year-old boy, Oscar, who's infatuated with his adult cousin Roger and daydreams that they'll run away together to lead a storybook life full of adventure. One afternoon at Green Beach, Roger encourages this fantasy. Roger tells Oscar that he'll need to pick up survival skills if the two of them want a shot at making it on their own: How to gut and scale a fish, how to skin a deer. When Roger runs out of beer — he's been drinking all day — he drives to the market, leaving Oscar alone at the beach. Oscar waits and waits, but Roger never returns. Close to midnight, Oscar accepts that his cousin isn't coming back and that Roger isn't worthy of his adoration.

What made Langley famous were the compulsion dramas, in which he took an ephemeral thought or urge and followed through to a logical-yet-extreme conclusion. Many compulsion dramas were intentionally unrealistic, even fantastical.

In "While You Were Out," a man takes a sedative after a root canal and falls into a deep sleep. His wife, watching over him, feels a sudden, irresistible desire to pluck one of his white hairs, which blossoms into an almost Ahab-like commitment to totally depilate him. She starts with a tweezer, upgrades to clippers, and then resorts to a razor. By the time he wakes up, she's shaved off all his head and facial hair. "You'll look better once you've had a little sun" is the last sentence.

In "Baby Crazy," an old maid — Langley's term, not mine — folding clothes at the laundromat finds a tiny white T-shirt that must belong to someone's infant. She writes a lost-and-found ad — *Missing something? Baby tee, newly washed* — which her pretty young neighbor answers. It's her daughter's. She must have left it in the dryer by mistake. The old maid dreams about the T-shirt that night and realizes that she desperately wants a child of her own. So she assembles a miniature wardrobe and kidnaps the neighbor's girl.

Line by line, Langley didn't offer much. He wasn't a great prose

stylist. Nor was he a deep thinker. He rarely fleshed out his characters' motives and provided only the briefest glimpses of their interi-
ority (the old maid wants a child). Like a behaviorist, he generally
confined himself to describing observable actions. His stories were
often extremely short, sometimes only a few pages long, and I wondered if that was because he didn't have much to say. Yet I warmed to
the material. Langley was versatile, by turns crude, exuberant, and
quiet. He could write by numbers—as in the simplistic epiphanies—
but he could also veer off trail. And after spending so many years in a
classroom, I appreciated that he seemed unambitious.

Browsing through the stacks, I found a copy of *The Encyclopedia of Twentieth-Century Literature*, which had a short paragraph on
Langley.

> Langley, Frederick (1938–1981). American short-story
> writer born in Concord, Mass. Released his debut
> collection, *Brutality and Delicacy* (1960), while an
> undergraduate at Faber College. Published two more
> collections in quick succession: *Alone at Green Beach* (1962)
> and *Omega* (1964), which cemented his reputation as a
> short-form master. Although popular with the public
> from the start, not recognized by critics until *Omega*.
> Died in a car accident.

Three books at two-year intervals, then nothing in the last sev-
enteen years of his life. That struck me as odd. Since no one had
gotten around to writing Langley's cradle-to-grave biography—
as a short-form rather than long-form master generally considered
more fun than important, he probably wasn't at the top of anyone's

list — I settled for something called *Freddy Remembered*, a slim oral history published in 1990.

On the inside flap I found a black-and-white head shot captioned simply *The author, 1963*. Langley had long wavy hair, a delicate nose, and an unusually pronounced supraorbital ridge. I tried, and failed, to think of a word to describe his gaze that wasn't *piercing* or *penetrating;* and I tried, and failed, to find in Langley's face some trace, however faint, of his niece.

The introduction claimed that "the people who knew Freddy best" had sat for interviews, which were then cobbled together into short "remembrances." There was no contribution from Helen Langley or, for that matter, anyone with the last name Langley, which arguably put the "best" into question. Oh, well. A common refrain was that the author found writing amazingly easy.

> Paul Church: I was editor of the Faber College *Beagle* when Freddy was a freshman. He started submitting stories as soon as he arrived on campus, and I liked them. They had a dashed-off quality. I don't mean that as an insult — better to say they seemed effortlessly produced, as in fact they were. He had that kind of genius. He found ideas everywhere. On a walk or listening to the radio. The joke on campus was that while other writers labored, Freddy's manuscripts arrived fully formed, delivered by stork. In the course of an afternoon, he could set down a whole story.
>
> He barely revised. When we first worked together I suggested improvements. But he found

the editing process frustrating. He didn't like going back to a story. We got into a fight once because I called him lazy. Freddy said, "I'm not lazy, I'm accepting." I think he meant that he didn't put on airs. He knew what he was capable of and what he was *not* capable of, and he didn't see the point in striving. I thought he was dead wrong and that there most certainly was a point. In the end, it was Freddy who got his way.

Rebecca Johnson: I dated Freddy when he was finishing up *Omega*. He was a really affectionate guy and he always had time for me. That was a surprise. I'd been with artists before and they always wanted whole weeks to themselves so they could work. "Becky, if you don't let me be, I'll never finish!" "Becky, get out of here, you're ruining my career!" It was like they needed a hundred hours of absolute silence just to get a few words on the page. Not Freddy Langley. He wanted to go out and have some fun. He loved going to fancy restaurants and ordering for everyone at the table so he could taste a bit of every dish. One time a waiter thought he was a food critic and gave us all free chocolate cake.

I did see Freddy in a dark mood this one time when he had to go see his dad. He said he had to "kiss the ring," which I guess was a reference to the Mob, which was strange because his dad was the headmaster at a religious school. Afterward he was in an even worse mood. He said his dad, who at first wasn't too pleased about the writer thing, was finally coming around. Freddy's dad saw that Freddy was doing well, making money, getting his name out. Everyone likes success, right? The way Freddy's dad saw it, if writing was what Freddy did best, and he was good at it, and he could earn a living at it, there was no harm in it. I was confused. "Shouldn't you be relieved, Freddy? Shouldn't you be happy he feels that way?" Freddy sneered.

Andrew Cafferty: In October of 1963 — I remember the month because the Dodgers had just swept the Yankees in the World Series — I threw a dinner party at my country house in Maine and I invited Freddy. I'd recently returned a pair of boots to L. L. Bean, the retail company, and was extolling their great customer service. I'd had the boots for eight or ten years already, but when I told the salesclerk that they were letting in water, he gave me another pair, no trouble at all. I guess I was going on.

All of a sudden Freddy stood up and declared he had an idea that he couldn't let get away. He demanded a pen, paper, and privacy.

In the morning — he'd spent the whole night writing — he came downstairs with "Lifetime Warranty," the famous story about a woman who purchases her husband from L. L. Bean via mail-order catalog and then returns him decades later

because he no longer satisfies her. You know,
sexually. That was the husband's "design flaw." He
"did not perform as advertised."

October 1963. Langley's final collection, which contained "Life-time Warranty," came out in September 1964. Assuming Andrew Cafferty had the date right and building in book-production lag time, then "Lifetime Warranty" must have been among the last stories that Langley completed for publication. I skipped ahead to the remembrance from Langley's book editor. He also mentioned "Lifetime Warranty."

Richard Anders: The highbrow crowd mostly
ignored Freddy, I suppose because he was popular.
There's nothing they despise more, you see. But
they loved "Lifetime Warranty."

Marxists claimed that Freddy was critiquing
capitalism and the way a profit-motivated society
teaches men and women to treat each other like
objects. Feminists read it as an empowering revenge
story. Women have needs too. Women should
realize that they, too, have the right to discard
unsuitable partners. Choosy selfishness isn't just for
men anymore! Loyalty is a feudalist hang-up! The
New Critics obsessed over a single line describing
the husband's outfit: "George wore his navy and
mountain red Norwegian sweater, which Alice had
given him on their first date, and which he had never
liked." It didn't sound like much, they admitted, but

it was the only time Freddy had chosen to give the husband's point of view — shared his feelings. What did it mean? It had to mean something!

Freddy found the whole "Lifetime Warranty" mania funny, because he'd intended the story to be just that: funny. "It's too much," he said, laughing. "I wrote it all in one night and I've never even read any Marx." The enthusiasm for "Lifetime Warranty" took me aback as well. I didn't say this to Freddy, but I didn't think the story was all that refined. It was a good read for a train ride. A trifle.

Richard Anders was naive — oddly so for an editor. He didn't seem to realize that critical feeding frenzies often had little to do with the objective quality of the work in question. If a story could be used to promote a pet construct, nothing else mattered. Not its heft. Not its finesse. Nothing, including the author's intentions. Langley had never read Marx. The Marxists did not care.

I looked for remembrances of Langley's later years, but his friends and professional acquaintances, the people who knew him best, knew him exclusively as a young man. There was only one entry concerning Langley's life after publishing.

Daniel Godolphin: I was living in Paris when Freddy was there, and we got along. We'd hang out at cafés and kid around. He listened to me complain about how much cheaper the city had been when Hemingway and those people were doing the expatriate thing. They could get by pretty nicely on the peanuts they got for their stories. On one occasion I worked up the guts to ask, "How much did *you* get for your stories?" I may have had a few too many drinks. He may have had a few too many drinks. He was annoyed. He wouldn't say. I'm pretty sure, though, that he got more than peanuts. It's weird he didn't keep churning that stuff out. If I'd had a major-league New York publisher and a fawning audience, I would've milked that situation. But I never saw him so much as sit down at a typewriter. I don't think he even brought one with him overseas.

Once a cub reporter tracked Freddy down with a magazine profile in mind. The reporter needled him: "Are you working on anything? More short stories? A novel? A screenplay?" Freddy kept saying no, but the reporter didn't take him at his word. He assumed he was hiding something, and he suggested that in his article. It was ridiculous. Freddy started getting letters from people back home saying, "When can we expect your great work?" It made him uncomfortable. He'd been inspired once, but he wasn't inspired anymore.

A Cliché

Again I walked to Worcester Square. Again Helen greeted me shoeless at the front door. This time she'd expected me. Again she led me to the den, and again she left me there alone, this time while she finished cooking. I took in the room like a familiar place, or, more precisely, with the wonder one feels at finding a place familiar that so recently seemed alien. How quickly one goes from *What's all this?* to *Oh, this.* Resting on the window ledge were unopened letters from multiple credit-card companies and a copy of Margaret Mitchell's *Gone with the Wind*. Its pages were yellow and its dustcover worn. COPYRIGHT MCMXXXVI BY THE MACMILLAN COMPANY.

Helen returned to find me reading the racist classic.

"Um," she said, infusing that one syllable with a heap of disapproval.

"Sorry. This must be for work, a look-but-don't-touch type of situation. Is it a first edition?"

"No, no, dear. That's not actually from 1936. It's a facsimile. I'm pleased, though, that you fell for it."

"There's a dark side of antiquarianism, I guess."

"Some clients don't care about the real thing. All they want is an impressive-seeming library."

"And do those clients know they're not buying the real thing?"

"I wouldn't dream of deceiving anyone."

Was she winking at me?

"The trickery's all on their end, not yours," I said.

"I disapprove. It's just—I have bills to pay. And rent. When I see an opportunity, I take that opportunity."

That statement may well have been a red flag, but I had enough at stake to ignore it. In Langley I had discovered precisely what Professor Davidoff had commanded me to seek: A subject for an inspirational case study. He was prolific, then silent. Inspired, then—there was no antonym for *inspired*. *Blocked. Dried up. De-inspired.* For Langley's process as a young man, I had *Freddy Remembered*. For the later years, I needed Helen. She was a primary source enfleshed. When I saw an opportunity, I took that opportunity.

I followed Helen into the sitting room, which doubled as a dining room. We arranged ourselves on either side of a foldout table that was usually a resting place for papers but now held our meal: spaghetti with red sauce on mismatched plates.

As if it mattered what she served. There were some authors—Mitchell among them—who could build a scene around food. They found significance in under-buttered rolls and improperly folded napkins; they found lyricism in crisp baguettes, soft white cheese, dry red wine, and the dry witticisms exchanged over that dry red wine. I guessed they were slow eaters—how else could they have observed so much?—whereas I consumed so quickly that I didn't really notice anything except, in this particular case, that the cook had used too much salt and that my dining companion was a partisan of the spoon-support technique for pasta. When

I was learning how to feed myself, no one had suggested that method and it still seemed exotic, more foreign than chopsticks.

I so looked forward to eating; not just at Helen's, in general. But eating itself was routinely disappointing because it never lasted long enough and the end was always in sight, always quantifiable: ten more bites, five more bites, two more bites, maybe three if I was careful. The period of satiation was painfully brief. Then began the countdown to the next feeding. Hours spent waiting for lunch, and then minutes to consume it. Hours spent waiting for dinner, and then a few more minutes to consume it.

Cooking anything in the least bit complicated came to seem futile, as silly as and perhaps sillier than spending money — which everyone said was the same as time — on an outfit I would wear only once. The outfit, once worn, would find its way to a closet and later a trash heap. The meal, once eaten, would find its way to a toilet and later a sewer. For these reasons I subsisted mostly on Pop-Tarts.

All that said, it was pleasant to have a hot meal for a change, and someone to talk to across the table, someone who listened patiently as I described, in greater detail than was strictly necessary, my usual dining habits, which I compared to my family's more formal habits when I was young. Back home, we'd eaten well and we'd eaten carefully, with two or three forks and two or three knives and the water glass and the wineglass placed just so, the multiple courses brought out just when. I felt a little guilty, a little ashamed of my casual degeneracy, but Helen laughed away my concerns. She had a full laugh. A warm, soothing, affirming, seductive laugh, nothing like Evelyn's high-pitched giggle, Evan's conceited guffaw, or Professor Davidoff's silent shoulder-shake.

Degeneracy, to Helen, was just another word for *liberation*. I should do exactly as I pleased. It was absurd to do anything else. Although she wished I were more capable of enjoying something so simple as food.

"Don't worry that it's futile, dear," she said, helping me to seconds. "Most things are."

We let the dishes fester and retired to a lumpy couch in the same room. Helen fetched a family photo album, one of those old-fashioned, leather-bound books filled with self-adhesive pages that had lost much of their stick. The spine read *Milford*, the Connecticut town where Helen had grown up. Side by side we waded in. On the first page were pictures of baby Helen crying, smiling, eating, crawling, sleeping, pointing at wooden toys—the gamut of infant actions—held aloft, held in arms, held on laps, thrown high into the air. She'd been an ugly baby: scrawny, bald, and splotchy.

"That's my father, Thomas," Helen said of a fair-skinned man looking out of the frame as little Helen tugged on his sleeve. "He was a psychiatrist. And my mother, Edith, who stayed at home." She was the standard white middle-class housewife, from the updo to the pumps. "My nanny, Valeria"—a Latin lady in a cornflower-blue apron. "She made me hot chocolate with marshmallows every day after school, using milk, whole milk, never water. And my grandfather, my paternal grandfather, Robert"—scowling, wild hair, thin face. "He lived not too far away, in Concord, where my father and Freddy were raised. My father got along with Robert well, he took after him, but he was a difficult man, extremely demanding. Anyway, I guess I'm boring you. You said you wanted to learn more about Freddy, so let's skip to the Freddy years. My uncle wasn't around when I was small."

"He must have been in Europe then," I said, drawing on my library research.

She nodded, neither surprised nor impressed by my knowledge.

"I met him when I was about fourteen. Well, I'd met him as a newborn but I don't remember that." Helen chuckled. "He came to visit, thinking he'd stay just a short while to get his bearings. He'd run out of money. But he never left."

"I didn't realize he lived with you."

"Right up until he died, about four years. Though I was at boarding school for part of that time."

Langley—I couldn't bring myself to call him Freddy, not even in my thoughts—did not seem eager to smile for the camera. His longish hair had gone gray. Not a nice gray either, more like wet-squirrel color. Broken capillaries crept across his nose.

"Well?" Helen asked.

"What?"

"Well, don't we look alike?"

They did not.

"Yes, the similarity is striking."

Helen beamed, flashing her sharp little teeth.

"Here's one where you can really see the family resemblance. Our nose and ears are just the same."

Judging from Langley's dazed expression, he'd been surprised by the photographer. He sat on his unmade bed, legs extended, back against a pillow, a beer resting precariously on his lap, wearing a yellow short-sleeved shirt open at the collar. Slovenly. There was something strange about the proportions of the space around Langley, at least as captured on film.

"The ceiling looks slanted," I said.

"He slept in the attic. My parents offered him a perfectly nice spare room. But he chose up there. He was a cliché."

She stated this matter-of-factly, as if it were a perfectly ordinary way to describe a human being. He was a baseball fan. He was a journalist. He was a father of three. He was a cliché.

"I'm not sure what you mean."

"How much do you know about my uncle, Anna?" she asked.

"Whatever's in *Freddy Remembered*."

"In that case, you know next to nothing. No one in my family had any interest in working with an official biographer — so nosy! — much less participating in a trivial oral history. The people rustled up for that collection — their impressions were stuck in the 1960s," she said bitterly. "They thought of him as a gifted college boy. By the time he moved in with my parents, he was washed up. I don't mean to sound harsh. I loved him. He was nice to me. He doted on me, gave me pocket money. Even as a girl, though, I could tell something was off. He'd stay cooped up in the attic for days at a time. Do you understand? That's what I mean when I say he was a cliché."

Helen kept flipping pages. Langley in front of a birthday cake, grinning and bearing it; Langley and Thomas playing cards, grinning and bearing it; Thomas mowing the lawn with Langley looking on from the front steps, grinning and bearing it. Langley's lackluster attitude prompted me to ask the question that had been nagging at me since the library.

"Why did your uncle stop writing after *Omega*?"

"He didn't."

"But—"

"He didn't. Well, for a long while he did. He'd just had enough, as far as I could tell. Then he started again. He kept notebooks. I figured you knew. I figured that was part of why you were here."

There were two notebooks, Helen told me. Langley had started the first in 1978, when he'd been living in the attic for twelve or fifteen months. It contained ideas, outlines, scattered thoughts. He'd started the second notebook not long before he died. It contained the rough draft of a longer project. Both notebooks were now in the possession of the university's rare-books library, the Elston, about a mile away from where we sat. But they weren't available for public consumption because Helen claimed they belonged to her and had sued the library to establish her rightful ownership.

"Anyone who wants to study the notebooks needs my permission until the courts sort this out," she said. "Only a small handful of people have read them—including me, naturally, but that was years ago and I don't remember much. All I can say definitively about the notebooks is that they're mine."

I could hardly believe my luck: Inspired, de-inspired, re-inspired. The fifty dollars I'd given Helen at the supermarket was starting to look like the best investment I'd ever made.

Helen announced that now was as fine a time as any to show me a letter from her uncle that was "very revealing." She led me through the house to her bedroom, which faced a patch of concrete that an ambitious broker might have called a backyard. It was spartan: a bed, a nightstand with a cheap metal lamp, a dresser and mirror. That was all. No plants or art. No personal touch. I loitered at the door, feeling awkward about entering Helen's retreat while she knelt beside the dresser and opened the bottom drawer.

Helen knew precisely where to find what she was looking for. Without hesitation she fished out a postcard displaying a sunny Connecticut beach — Hammonasset — with the Connecticut motto, *Qui transtulit sustinet*. "He who is transplanted still sustains." On the back, in messy cursive: *Dear Helen, Remember what we talked about. Love, Freddy.*

I returned the cryptic postcard to my host. She received it carefully with both hands, like a raw egg or a football.

"Let me explain," said Helen, reading my thoughts. She sat on the bed and I leaned against the door frame. "One day at boarding school, the headmistress interrupted my math class to say that my uncle was on the phone; he wanted to speak to me urgently. I could tell immediately that he was in a bad state. Anxious. Morbid. He said, 'I need you to promise me something.' 'Anything, Freddy.' He said — his exact words — 'When I'm gone, I want you to look after my notebooks.' I never did find out what set him off, but I promised to do as instructed. Then he sent me this postcard. It's evidence that the notebooks are mine."

Helen still held the postcard with both hands. She gripped it chest-high, reminding me of grief-stricken survivors in post-disaster newscasts who so hopefully exhibit head shots of their probably deceased loved ones. To Helen, the postcard was evidence, but for it to carry any weight, one would have to believe that she faithfully recalled a conversation that had taken place decades earlier. I did believe her. If her lawsuit rested on so little, however, it was hopeless. The presiding judge wouldn't have heard her laugh, wouldn't have eaten her salty pasta on an empty stomach accustomed to Pop-Tarts, wouldn't have any good reason to trust her.

"How'd the Elston end up with the notebooks?"

"Freddy died unexpectedly, as you might already know."

"In a car accident."

"Right." She nodded. "It fell to my parents to handle the funeral, which was a nightmare, as you can imagine. They also had to dispose of all his stuff—as they saw it, all his junk. The easiest option was to ask the Salvation Army to pack up the attic, just take everything away." Helen paused. She played with her hair. "It happened so fast, I didn't have a chance to find the notebooks. I figured some idiot had thrown them out along with Freddy's old sweaters and tennis shoes. But I was wrong. A few years ago, they turned up at an estate sale, and a curator from your university swooped in."

Not for the first time, my university was taking a finders-keepers approach to cultural patrimony. It was a Collegiate professor who'd raided Tiwanaku and returned home with a truckload of artifacts: ceramics, jewelry, human skeletons. A century later, Collegiate was still insisting that its claim to Bolivia's national treasure was as good as Bolivia's.

"May I ask what it is you're doing?" Helen said.

Unthinkingly, I'd fallen into my stretching routine. Arms up; chest out. I must have looked ridiculous. When I explained that my rhomboids hurt, Helen offered to rub my back. Or more like ordered me to sit on the bed so she could do so. She stood above me, using her thumbs to circle and press my sore muscles. At first the physical intimacy made me self-conscious. But the pleasure of relief banished that feeling quickly. Through some mysterious pathway in my nervous system, every pinch along my spine made my earlobes tingle.

"I'll give permission for you to read the notebooks if you want," she said. "I don't mind. You have to go through the Elston, and then they send the request to my lawyer. It takes a little while. Maybe your adviser can help speed things up on the university side."

The Notebook

Veronica Lancet was not my first kiss. Moira
Christiansen, the busty Norwegian, was my first kiss,
a few months earlier in her backyard. A warm spring
day. Smelled of lilac and salt. Thomas was there,
watching us. I half remember him mocking me
afterward with the extreme cruelty that only a big
brother could muster. Did Moira's tongue feel like wet
fruit, or did Veronica's? *Wet fruit* is a little imprecise
and I must remember to choose my words more
carefully. I mean *papaya*. There was no ice-cube-in-
hot-tea effect with Moira, which must be why she
slipped my mind.

Jordan is an editor at a fancy Manhattan magazine.
His job is to place words next to ads, but he believes
he's an artist who works with artists. An artist who
works at making artists better at their art. A
wordsmith. A carver of language. A butcher of useless
adverbs. His young assistant, Allen, is less
pretentious. He gets that he works in advertising, and
he has a knack for pleasing the moneymen. No, he
won't assign a critical piece on a horrifically unsafe car

when GM is paying for placement. Yes, he will send an ambitious imbecile to the fancy new West African hotel owned and operated by a brutal dictator. The publisher loves Allen. Slowly, Allen usurps Jordan's place. Jordan believes this is the triumph of venal bullshit shallow capitalism over solemn Art and rigorous Craft. Is it?

A man walks into a dark bar in the middle of the afternoon. It takes a minute for his eyes to adjust. There's something wrong. Something eerie, something uncanny, about this place. Is it the place, come to think of it, or the clientele? There's something familiar about the people in it. He recognizes all of them but he doesn't know from where. One man winks at him. He has a nose like a beak with cavernous oval nostrils. He has thick, thick eyebrows and dark, dark eyes. Wait, he looks a lot like that guy what's-his-name who played Moon in *The Seven-Ups*. Yes! Our protagonist examines more carefully his fellow drinkers. They're all character actors. That guy who always plays a corrupt cop. That other guy who always plays a corrupt cop. That guy from *The Longest Yard*. It's a convention for the famous-but-not-known.

Flouncing around a cocktail party, Delores amuses herself by pretending she's a fashion reporter. She describes (to herself) Adam's white linen shirt with mother-of-pearl buttons. Elaine's blue suede flats with long toe boxes. Nick's black leather briefcase with gold-plated locks. Lawrence's alligator-skin belt with a copper buckle. Oh, look, Lawrence missed a loop in the back. I want the reader to assume that, in this universe, clothing and accessories are significant, imbued with meaning—that the characters' sartorial choices say something about their personalities. They do not. There is no relationship. The story is a trap for readers.

Frank Luce writes a successful debut novel that's turned into a blockbuster film. He makes so much money, just gobs and gobs of it, he knows he will never need to work again. But he's embarrassed to let on that he intends to spend the rest of his life doing nothing. (Something seeming superfluous.) So he pretends he's suffering from writer's block.

Luce understands that the desire to do nothing is shocking to Americans. In surveys, most people call themselves "middle class," and for all the political rhetoric about rewarding wealth, Americans find the notion of someone rich enough not to lift a finger not only repulsive but also confusing. It seems wrong. Morally hand-on-the-Bible wrong. It seems European. God forbid anyone with means takes a rest before turning sixty-five. Those with money must either make more money or assist those without. There are no other options.

I mean North Americans. Brazilians are different.

Using writer's block as a beard, Luce makes his avocation (leisure) his vocation (leisure). Edmund Bergler coined the term *writer's block* in 1947. (So says my handy *Britannica*. Well, not mine; Helen's.) Bergler said writer's block could be total or partial and that it grew out of "feelings of insecurity." He traced these feelings to "oral masochism" and a "superego-driven need for punishment."

I barely understand what that goddamn fool means.

Bergler thought writers starved themselves creatively because their mothers had starved them of milk during breast-feeding. Pardon me? Hilarious. At dinner parties, Luce complains loudly that his mother never breast-fed him. Too much? She'd tear her nipple away from precious little Franky and he'd cry and cry.

Life-Hacking

Helen was wearing makeup this time, too much of it. Too-red lipstick, too-thick mascara, green eye shadow, blush. When she smiled at me, I thought of Aschenbach with his painted face leering at Tadzio. I was a little older than Tadzio, sure, but Helen and Aschenbach were probably rounding the same decade. Maybe Helen was under the impression that we were on a date? But the context was thoroughly unromantic. She couldn't possibly have misunderstood my plea for company as a bid for companionship.

The atmosphere in the auditorium, a large black box with stadium seating, approximated a synagogue before a bris. Anticipatory yet wary. In the front were athletic-looking men — business students. Behind them were a few architects, easily identified by their blatant exhaustion and knit wool ties. I noticed emissaries from the law school and the medical school, but I was the only English PhD. No Evan, Evelyn, or anyone else. Professor Davidoff, apparently, was alone in thinking his ward could use time-management advice. The other advisers had more confidence in their protégés.

Helen and I had only just selected our seats when a tall

bottle-blonde in a tight navy dress and navy high heels approached the lectern. Really high heels, not just flats with a little boost. A business professor, I presumed, who wanted to show her honored guest that although higher education was a refuge for the sartorially challenged, it was not only that. Her hair color and outfit sang to me unreasonably; they seemed to hold a semiotic charge. They told me how frustrating it was to live among people who did not share one's values and yet knew that the world at large *did* share those values, *did* subscribe to the notion that one ought to dress for the job one wanted, not the job one had, et cetera.

She — this priest among atheists in a God-fearing country — murmured into the microphone, provoking shouts of "Louder!"

"Excuse me, I'm not used to this sort of thing," she said, and suddenly the dress seemed more like a shield than a cassock.

She paused to arrange her notes. As always happened in such moments, students shifted in their seats and coughed into their elbows. Helen coughed too. Silence inevitably causes coughing in crowded auditoriums. It is a reflex. Finally the woman spoke up, filling the already hot, stale room with hot, stale, fatuous praise.

"Please join me in welcoming our guest, the *New York Times* bestselling author Francis Goodman. *Forbes* once called him 'the most efficient man in the world' and the editors of *Fortune* magazine twice included him on their annual fifty-entrepreneurs-under-fifty list. I could go on. But if I went on, Mr. Goodman would accuse me of wasting time."

Halfhearted laughter. Applause. White guy, black hair, black frame glasses, black jeans, black sweater, black plastic watch: the uniform of the new economy. A booming voice that seemed all the more oppressive after the professor who wasn't used to this sort of thing, because Goodman was undoubtedly used to this sort of thing.

"My high-school guidance counselor used to say that moving up in life takes grit, determination, and patience. Moving up in life is like climbing Mount Everest." Here Goodman left the podium, jumping more than stepping down, as if escaping an assailant. He walked along the edge of the stage. "Is that a good metaphor? I think not. More than one person can get to the top. The prize is the summit. And if you hire the right Sherpa, you'll get there, whether it takes you two weeks or a month to arrive. Hundreds of people do it every year. That's a fact. Look it up if you don't believe me. But you kids are smart; I bet you've guessed where I'm going with this. If hundreds of people can climb up Everest every year, then Everest tells us nothing about what it takes to climb up the corporate ranks. Is there a company in this country with hundreds at the summit, the C suite? Can anyone name one? No? That's because no such company exists. One chief executive officer per firm, folks, that's the American way." Goodman stopped pacing to better stare at the crowd. The modern workplace was not like Everest, he told us. The modern workplace was like the Indianapolis 500. "You're on the same track with your competitors. You're all doing the exact same thing: going around in circles. But one man, or woman, will finish his, or her, laps ahead of everyone else. How does he do it?" he went on, abandoning gender equity. "He's tough — but everyone is tough. He has a good car — but everyone has a good car. So how does he do it? He takes the turns faster. He's more efficient."

Helen's knee brushed against mine. Once she had my attention, she rolled her eyes.

Goodman kept on explaining why working in an office was just like racing cars and not at all like climbing a tall mountain, although he never bothered to support his basic argument: that efficiency was key to both finishing first in the Indianapolis 500 and becoming a CEO. Whether he thought efficiency was also instrumental in finishing a dissertation, he did not say. "Efficiency is paramount," he said repeatedly.

At last Goodman retook the podium to share the life-hacking tips that had made him famous. He dispensed these in a firm tone of voice, as if revealing holy wisdom. Sleeping in, he said, was immoral. One should wake up no later than six o'clock — Goodman woke up at five o'clock — and immediately "down" a large glass of water. "If all you're doing at breakfast is eating, you're doing it wrong," he said. At breakfast, one should compose a list of goals to accomplish by noon, four, and close of business. Sitting was unhealthy. On the off chance we hadn't already thrown away our office chairs, we should do so immediately and instruct our human resources departments to purchase standing desks. The Varidesk Pro, Goodman said, was the best on the market.

Helen sighed audibly as Goodman expelled increasingly exotic ideas for how to enhance productivity. Goodman recommended drinking energy shakes in the shower. He suggested exercising while at the office through "walking meetings." Why sit at a conference table when you can pace the hallways? "The hallways are your treadmills." Around three, a coffee break was advisable. *Break*, though, was merely a figure of speech. A coffee break was an opportunity to problem-solve in the fresh context of a café or corporate cafeteria. New surroundings would help in generating ideas. So would caffeine. In case brilliance descended between sips, Goodman exhorted us to always keep a laptop handy. He stressed that we must "utilize every moment."

Afterward we went to my apartment. A little rattled by its grandeur, Helen scraped her winter boots meticulously on the welcome mat. She'd expected me to live in a grungy dorm, not the second floor of the Roosevelt—a red-brick, Colonial Revival building on the green that was as close to luxury accommodations as one could find downtown. It was an old New Harbor sort of place, originally a hotel, and back when famous people used to come through the city—Woodrow Wilson, Andrew Mellon, Calvin Coolidge, Albert Einstein, Babe Ruth, and Horace Dutton Taft—this was where they stopped.

Helen joked that Collegiate's graduate-student stipends were clearly more lavish than she had imagined, prompting me to confess that my deceased grandfather had paid, indirectly, for the lease as well as everything inside the apartment. She asked for a tour. Still in her orange coat, she inspected my framed achievements: high-school diploma, college diploma, a letter from my college dean recognizing my "extraordinary grades," et cetera. The blank space, I explained, would one day show off my PhD. Facing my self-portrait were Russian political posters from the Stalinist period that extolled the delights of factory work and instructed laborers to look out for wheat thieves (big-nosed Jew-y types). As my medical-school friend had remarked before *Baise-moi* tore us asunder, it was just as tasteless to display Soviet propaganda as Nazi propaganda; more than two million people had died in Stalin's gulags. I knew that, but I kept the posters anyway. They looked bold, I thought, in the otherwise bland sitting room with two identical black-leather-and-steel Le Corbusier sofas, one on either side of a kidney-shaped glass coffee table.

I led Helen to my bedroom and pointed out the solitary item that my grandfather had bought directly: my desk. It — my bedroom — was the nicest room in the apartment, with its large window overlooking the green, but it was unloved. Three dust bunnies rested on the blue Persian carpet, an indication of my poor housekeeping skills. (And the fact that I hadn't bothered to call the cleaners in a while.) My bed was unmade. Our coats, tossed carelessly on top of it, mingled with the sheets. My window curtains were filthy. The pile of old *New Yorker* magazines on the floor was preposterously high. A long time ago I'd stopped reading the articles, and then I'd stopped paging through them for the cartoons, and then I'd stopped checking the table of contents, which often had been just enough for me to affect familiarity with current intellectual affairs.

When we returned to the Le Corbusier sofas, I opened a bottle of red wine for us to share. Helen's lipstick stained her glass, though not conspicuously since the color had faded in the past few hours. Once again I apologized — I'd done so right after Goodman shut up — for inviting her to such an inane talk, which wasn't particularly useful to my professional pursuits and so, I assumed, even less to hers.

"Maybe the JDs in the audience will get ahead with walking meetings and all that," I said, "but none of his tips seemed relevant to me. Half the professors in my department have had hip-replacement surgery. And if the practical advice was actually impractical, the overall message was just obvious: Work hard, work constantly, make the most of your interstitial time, like your morning shower, use it to get ahead. It was interesting sociologically, though," I continued. "Goodman's successful because he gets that rich people don't have any time. It's one of those modern incongruities, like how the poor are fat and the rich are thin. The richer you get, the fewer vacations you take, the more work you do."

"I'm not sure the people in coal mines would agree," Helen said piously.

"Yeah, O.K.," I replied. "I realize there's a difference between office labor and manual labor. But lawyers at corporate firms log twelve-hour days and take almost no vacation. That's not the case in coal mines. Unions wouldn't allow it."

"Why is that, do you think? Not the union rules. I mean, why do rich people work so hard?"

"What choice do they have?"

"That's just it. They do have a choice. They're already rich. If I had money, I'd do nothing at all," she said. "I'm serious. Everyone would be better off if the rich took it easy. Think of all those trust-fund kids toiling away at banks, making money they don't need off other people's backs, inflating their resources at some needy person's expense."

"The economy, to you, is a zero-sum game. When the rich play, they mess it up for everyone."

"No offense intended."

"None taken. Trust me, I'm not inflating my resources. I'm

depleting them. Somehow, even though I don't have what you might call a life, I spend a lot more than I take in."

"Good. If I were in your position, if I lived in a place like this, I'd just relax."

"Then everyone you knew would hound you. My parents think I relax too much. They say I'm lazy. My adviser does too. That's why he sent me to that life-hacking lecture — if I could just hack my life, I'd be able to finish my dissertation, or something."

I refilled Helen's glass and mine as well. Although I was no expert, it was obviously a nice wine. Bordeaux, Château Montrose, 1996. I'd taken the bottle from my parents' house when I'd last visited them.[1]

---

1   *Thanksgiving Day. Anna; her parents, Sarah and Michael; her uncle Joshua, and his wife, Nora, sit around a crowded table.*
    JOSHUA: More turkey please, Sarah.
    SARAH: Certainly, Joshua. Michael, could you help? It's too heavy for me. Anna, more for you?
    ANNA: No, thanks, Mom.
    MICHAEL: How about sweet potatoes? They're delicious.
    ANNA: No, thanks, Dad.
    MICHAEL: At least finish your plate. And sit up straight. You're bent over like a peasant.
    ANNA: All right, Dad.
    MICHAEL: You're still bent over like a peasant, and you wonder why your back always hurts.
    ANNA: My rhomboids.
    MICHAEL: Those are parts of your back, are they not?
    ANNA: Yes.
    SARAH: Let her be.
    MICHAEL: Ha, as if you ever —
    NORA: Well, I'll have some sweet potatoes. Thanksgiving is not a good day for diets. That's what I always say: It is not a good day for diets.
    ANNA: Has anyone ever said otherwise?
    MICHAEL: Anna.

SARAH: Joshua, I was so interested in what you were saying just now. What were you saying just now? I know it was interesting.

JOSHUA: I think, I think I was describing that terrible moment my first year in med school when I flunked my microbiology midterm.

SARAH: Dad was so upset.

JOSHUA: He was. He demanded to know what had gone wrong, and I couldn't really give him an explanation. I just couldn't keep my head down. I wanted to party and sleep in, have a good time. I couldn't stand the library. I told Dad, "I'm sick of school." He said, "You'll get through it." I said, "I won't." He said, "It's just a few more years. Then you'll be a doctor. It's worth it." I said, "I can't do it." He said, "You can."

SARAH: He brought up Dr. Barrington, didn't he?

MICHAEL: Who?

JOSHUA: Dr. Barrington. When I was a little boy I broke my ankle playing soccer and went to see Dr. Barrington. He gave me a lollipop and put me in a cast. He promised I'd get well in time for the next season, and I did. I was so grateful, and I said to myself, "I'm going to be a doctor. I'm going to heal people, just like Dr. Barrington." Why are you smirking?

ANNA: This is the way my face looks most of the time.

NORA: I think I need another glass of wine.

SARAH: Red or white? I recommend the red, a very fine bottle a decade old. We've been saving the case.

NORA: White — red gives me migraines.

JOSHUA: Ladies, please, I'm trying to talk to Anna.

ANNA: Oh? I thought we were having a general conversation. I thought you were just sharing this episode from your past with all of us for no particular reason.

JOSHUA: Dad said, "You've wanted to be a doctor ever since Dr. Barrington. Medicine is what you were meant to do."

SARAH: He believed in the concept of a calling.

ANNA: He did?

JOSHUA: His was business.

MICHAEL: Well, usury.

JOSHUA: Mine is medicine. Nora's is interior design. Your mother's, Anna, is fund-raising. Your father's is investment banking. Yours is —

ANNA: I get it.

JOSHUA: I never cared for reading myself, but it doesn't matter. The point is that you've always had a bookish inclination, better with words than people. Anyway, after Dad mentioned Dr. Barrington, I hung up the phone. I went back to partying and sleeping in. But it wasn't much fun anymore. There's nothing meaningful about laziness. There's something depressing, after a while, about letting your talent go to waste. Something childish.

SARAH: You have to maximize your potential.

ANNA: Who does?

SARAH: You do. Everyone does.

JOSHUA: Right. I didn't want to disappoint my past self, the little boy who wanted to be a doctor. I went back to school and I buckled down. That's all I had to do. That's all you have to do.

ANNA: What I do is different. All you had to do was memorize formulas.

JOSHUA: Not exactly.

ANNA: More or less. You didn't have to invent anything. You just had to learn.

MICHAEL: Invent? I thought your job was to tell people what books are about.

ANNA: Arguments are inventions.

MICHAEL: If you're having such a hard time, maybe you should consider doing something else. There's always law school.

JOSHUA: I thought about law school.

SARAH: You did?

JOSHUA: It seemed easier than medicine.

ANNA: I thought medicine was your calling?

JOSHUA: Yes, and when I reminded myself of that, med school wasn't so rough anymore. Well, I still had to huff and puff just to get Cs. And sometimes I'd try to concentrate but my mind would wander and I'd feel tempted to goof off.

MICHAEL: When that happens to me, I go for a jog, get the endorphins moving.

NORA: Oh, so do I! Exercise clears the mind.

JOSHUA: Sometimes I'd curse the day I decided to become a doctor.

SARAH: Joshua.

JOSHUA: The point is, it was all worth it. When I meet people at conferences now I can tell them, "I'm doing what I've always wanted to do. What I was meant to do."

The more I thought about it, the more I doubted that Goodman's central, obvious message — work hard if you want to succeed — was true when the goal was a dissertation, though Professor Davidoff and my family subscribed to it. Why should I believe that life-hacking would lead to degree completion? There was a difference between not writing a dissertation and not writing a satisfactory dissertation, wasn't there? Had anyone ever established — scientifically — a direct relationship between a strong work ethic and scholarly success?

A strong work ethic, probably, was to scholarly success what dental hygiene was to healthy teeth. That is to say, most people who brushed their teeth constantly and flossed constantly and never ate candy had no cavities. On the other end of the spectrum, most people who never brushed their teeth, never flossed, and constantly ate candy had a lot of cavities. Perhaps their teeth fell out. But in the murky middle were people who brushed once or twice a day and flossed once or twice a month. Some of those people had cavities; others did not. The x factor was genetics. What was the x factor in my profession? If I'd made a habit of waking up at five o'clock and drinking Red Bull in the shower, would I have finished my dissertation already? More likely I would have collapsed from exhaustion.

I said as much to Helen.

"Flossing and energy drinks. When you talk about what you do, it sounds like drudgery."

"It is," I said. "I'll feel happy when I finish my dissertation and my adviser tells me it's the greatest student scholarship he's ever read. I can't feel happy while it's in progress."

Helen laughed in her usual way, full and generous.

"When I found myself thinking like that, I dropped out of college. Did you know that I'm a college dropout? You've probably never had one in your house before, excluding the help. I'd already gone to a fancy boarding school and I figured I knew enough. I didn't want to keep delaying happiness. I was young, naive, but I think I did the right thing. I spent the best years of my life doing virtually nothing. In Italy. My uncle was the same way. He hated the kind of goal-oriented mind-set you're describing because he thought it left no room for pleasure."

"Hedonism meets Buddhism."

"No. Common sense. If you're doing something because you're expecting a reward, then you're not living in the here and now and you won't enjoy the action itself."

"But when the action is a chore, no one enjoys that."

"Freddy would have said that rewards, or payoffs, turn joyful activities into chores. Everything turns into flossing."

"Still, I don't see how that's a philosophy anyone can live by. To feel pleasure, I'd have to write a dissertation without any intention of submitting it for review. You'd have to, I don't know, bind books and never sell them, or bind books and then unbind them. Kant thought everyone had a duty to cultivate his talents. I guess your uncle would have found the emphasis on duty joy-destroying. But the alternative is to let your talent lie fallow and rot."

"Money's the deciding factor, in my opinion. If you have it, why not rot? If you don't, you've got to cultivate until you die."

On her way out that evening, Helen noted that I'd never deposited the fifty-dollar check she'd given me on Christmas and that this was a blessing, because her bank account was running low. In a show of friendship, I found the check and tore it up dramatically. Then I wrote a new one, for five hundred dollars, to get Helen through what she called a rough patch.

I went to my messy bed happy and self-satisfied. If I was willing to help a new friend without question or reservation, that had to mean I wasn't a particularly lousy addition to the human race. Arguably I was a good one. My altruism was heroic.

A Level of Incompetence

Campus towns give rise to weird establishments unlikely to survive in more normal environments, café-cum-bookstores, specifically the kind with a ludicrously allusive menu, being a prime example. At the New Harbor branch, every sandwich had a name and every name contained a literary reference. Ham and cheese: Hamingway and Cheese. Tuna salad: Melville's Tuna Fish-Mael. Each day at lunchtime serious and self-serious people walked into the café and said "Fish-Mael."

I'd found the café charming, initially. It had been a part of my routine when I was still embroiled in course work, the place I went with classmates to compare notes, debrief, mock whatever meager insight Evelyn had thought fit to share that day. In the months when I was studying for my oral exams, I would drop in almost daily for coffee and a pastry — after a jog, before a session at the library. Sometimes even twice daily if I needed a shot of espresso before a party. I couldn't remember if I'd stopped running before I'd stopped coming in for coffee, or stopped coming in for coffee before I'd stopped attending parties.

The orbit of my life was too confined now to include the café as a regular stop; often, it wouldn't even touch the library. I preferred the comfort of home, venturing out only for grocery trips or to distract myself from my word count. My occasional itch for human company was passably satisfied by inevitable contact with my classmates and my adviser. Speaking of: I'd returned to the café after a long absence because Professor Davidoff had summoned me there.

Professor Davidoff had not yet arrived.

Not hungry enough for a full meal, I ordered an apple-cinnamon toaster strudel — basically a fancy Pop-Tart — and sat at the table farthest from the glass door that did little to keep out the cold. Someone had left behind a copy of the *New Harbor Weekly*, the city's alternative rag.

Crime report: Muggings were on the rise again, especially around the edges of the university campus. A hit-and-run on Steeple Street left Egg, a cat, dead. Egg's brother Nog was visibly depressed. Did anyone have information about the racist graffiti in the alley by the Islamic student center? If so, contact the police.

Professor Davidoff was now fifteen minutes late for our meeting.

New Harbor Observed: Holiday decorations were still strewn around the city. It was common to the point of cliché to deride early Santas and Rudolphs who arrived when turkeys still rightly had dominion. The truly egregious problem, though, according to the paper's staff curmudgeon, was lingering, not prematurely. Droopy firs, burned-out string lights, Styrofoam snow reduced to rubble slush. Anticipation of Christmas was depressing because it implied emptiness at all other times, but at least dinner, gifts, and vacation lay ahead. Remembrance of Christmas had nothing to recommend it.

Feature: The city was planning to demolish — to implode —

the New Harbor Coliseum, which the local government and many community groups thought blighted downtown. It did. The author, however, was a sentimentalist who opposed the idea. He'd gone to shows at the coliseum as a teenager and thought the city should try to save it. He went on at some length about a Van Halen concert, the locus of his first kiss. The implosion was scheduled for late February, but an eleventh-hour public outcry could possibly save "the remarkable structure."

Still no Professor Davidoff.

I didn't care what they did to the New Harbor Coliseum, really, although it seemed a useful reminder of human stupidity and hubris. The city had spent millions of taxpayer dollars to build the thing—an unsuccessful ploy to bring suburbanites back to the area. Yet more taxpayer dollars would be spent getting rid of it.

What a pathetic excuse for a city. A superstitious person might have wondered if New Harbor was cursed, if a malignant genie, one provoked by well-laid plans, hovered over it. Countless times the city had tried to widen its influence, boost its income, only to find that the proposed agent of prosperity was in fact an agent of decline. The pattern started in the seventeenth century when Puritan zealots scraped together a boatload of goods to establish trade with England. But the ship never reached its destination. It disappeared. And this was catastrophic; months of labor lost just as Boston to the north and New Amsterdam to the south were developing their ports. New Harbor fell behind and never recovered.

Twenty-seven minutes late, Professor Davidoff sat across from me without apology. Since we were meeting at a café, not his office, he must have felt that punctuality wasn't strictly necessary. And he was taking advantage of the venue in other ways, having ordered an elaborate coffee concoction—consisting primarily of steamed milk—and a chocolate chip cookie. He dunked the latter into the former and left it there too long, so when he removed it, the bottom broke off, a soggy mess. He tried again. Wiser from experience, he dipped rather than dunked, then quickly transferred the cookie into his mouth to avoid a midair collapse. The speed at which he executed this procedure made him seem ravenous.

"The last time we talked, Anna," Professor Davidoff began at last, "you'll remember I pointed out that you'd fallen behind."

"I remember. You also told me to find a case-study author to ground my thesis—and I have."

The professor leaned back in his chair and grinned, revealing chocolate-stained teeth. The interval between white enamel and dark chocolate resembled a keyboard. *Pareidolia* was the word I hadn't managed to recall at New Campus Library, the one that meant seeing faces in a cloud.

"Who is it?"

"Frederick Langley."

The broad grin disappeared, his facial expressions repeating in a few seconds the multiyear arc of our relationship.

"He's a little juvenile, no?"

"*Accessible* is a better word. *Accessible,* at worst."

"That disgusting foreskin story—"

Unprepared to defend Langley's work, I dropped the matter of his reputation. (I'd felt quite the same as my adviser in the recent past, and I hadn't fully replaced my adolescent assessment with a mature one.) I argued instead that Langley was worth my while because he was de-inspired and then re-inspired. Even better, I had within my grasp an academic unicorn: the author's unpublished notebooks sitting in our very own rare-books library.

More precisely, they were just beyond my grasp. There was something fishy about the way the library had acquired the notebooks. There was drama. There was legal trouble. Long story short, the library couldn't make the notebooks available without permission from an attorney. Would Professor Davidoff play fixer, start the process with the Elston on my behalf? He would.

This molehill was mine. Redemption would soon follow. Of course it would.

Professor Davidoff already knew about the lawsuit, which he considered insignificant. "That woman, his cousin, has no case," he said. I didn't correct him. His tone of voice made me think I shouldn't disclose my connection to the plaintiff. "A judge should have ruled in our favor long ago but it's always tough with these relatives. Eventually our lawyers will wear her down. We have resources. She doesn't."

Professor Davidoff bought himself a second cookie. He bit into it lustily and peered fixedly at the remaining crescent while he chewed. Then he swallowed hard, broke off a new chunk of chocolate, and tossed it through his parted lips, like popcorn. Crumbs fell gently onto his dress shirt, like snow flurries or dandruff.

"Anna, before we had this conversation, I was starting to worry that you'd never listen to my advice. I was doubtful, frankly, that you'd ever settle down to finish your dissertation. And, frankly, I was going to suggest that you at least start thinking about — what else you might want to do."

"What?"

"I don't mean to insult you. You're a smart girl. When you first arrived, you were among my best students. I was sure you'd go far. I told other professors to look out for you. I even told my wife all about you. It's just, frankly, the Peter Principle, I suppose."

Between this last reference and Professor Davidoff's suggestion that I attend a life-hacking lecture, I wondered if he had a sideline in management theory. The Peter Principle, according to my adviser, states that employers select candidates for a new position based almost entirely on their performances in their current roles rather than on their suitability for the intended role—that is, on whether their abilities match the job requirements. Workers will therefore receive promotions until they reach a "level of incompetence."

"You're saying that writing a dissertation is my level of incompetence?"

"I'm saying make the most of these notebooks."

The Notebook

Funny to me the way Sherlock Holmes always gets his man in the end. Not *that* he gets him, but the way. It bothers me that it's impossible for the reader to guess what happened. I never see the answer coming. Usually, detective = reader, and criminal = writer, but Holmes is more of a writer, making things up as he goes along. So how can the actual reader keep up? No one could possibly figure out that "the band! The speckled band!" is a deadly Indian snake that climbed up a bell cord through a ventilator. Come on. What if: A detective story in that style. The detective makes astonishing leaps. The sidekick very impressed. In the end the detective apprehends a man and reveals the whole convoluted story. But wait: He's wrong. The man has an airtight alibi, had nothing to do with the crime. All the clues the detective thought he'd uncovered were figments of his imagination.

A world in which your parents die the instant you successfully reproduce. They've outlived their utility in a Darwinian sense, so why should they go on living at all? We must all choose between our children and our parents. So this lifelong bachelor believes. This lifelong bachelor whose mother took her exit long before his children, her grandchildren, were a biological possibility. I was four. Didn't even lose my virginity for another decade. Mother left only the haziest impression. Mostly I remember absence and howling, unfulfilled want. Come to think of it, I doubt she breast-fed me. Thomas might know.

Thomas said he does not know. Thomas said to ask Dad if I want to give him a stroke. There's an idea. Two down and no need to create life to take it. Thomas said to occupy my mind with more wholesome questions. He seems to find me beneath conversation. Monosyllables and reprimands are good enough for his little brother.

Alfred Watt commits the perfect crime. A theft of some sort, like a bank heist, and no one's the wiser. He keeps checking the papers to see if anyone's onto him, but no. Weeks go by. Months go by. Years go by. He turns himself in because he can't handle it anymore. He wants recognition. Finally the tabs take note. Proust said, "In matters of crime, where there is danger for the culprit, it is self-interest that dictates confessions; where the offense incurs no penalty, it is self-esteem." Does that apply? Let others judge. Will others judge? A silent confession incurs no judgment.

Tomato salad is the best salad, followed by Waldorf, potato, egg, and green. If it contains fish, it is not a salad, it is a mash or a scramble. If menus called it scrambled tuna with carrots, celery, and whipped egg yolks, no one would order it and the world would be a better place. When I explained this to Edith, she laughed. "It's not a joke," I said. "I'm serious." The next day she made me a tuna scramble on rye for lunch. I washed it down with six beers. I don't much like Edith. Not just because of the tuna. Is it really necessary to keep even the hallways spotless? At least she talks to me.

Another fight with Thomas. When I came home from Europe he embraced me like the prodigal son and assumed I was ready to change, to reform myself. I don't know where he got that idea. Finally he's beginning to understand that I never had and never will have, not in a million years or more, I can wait until the sun explodes, any interest in his narrow sort of wife-and-child-and-job life. Why, if it prosper, none dare call it life.

That meddlesome man in Paris asked me why once. Why was my career shaped like a cliff? Or why not, more like. Why not just keep going? David or Dennis. Last name like a sea creature. What a strange question, as if the most natural thing once you've started is to never stop.

The lecture Dad most liked to give was on the parable of the talents, which he preferred to the parable of the prodigal son, aka the parable of the loving father — ha. It made no sense to him that a father would reward a screwup offspring. The parable of the talents was easier for him to accept. A hard God for a hard man. Dad is a hard man, adamant and steel. Everyone in Concord revered him. He ran a tight ship, they said, at the school and at home too. Our neighbors assumed he thought up that "business-parenting" system of paying us pennies for every completed chore, which I hated and which so many of them adopted as a way to teach the value of work and money to their spoiled, post-Depression children. Nothing was ever done for its own sake. Everything had its reward, or its punishment. Actually, Dad got the idea from John D. Rockefeller.

For it will be like a man going on a journey, who called his servants and entrusted to them his property. To one he gave five talents, to another two, to another one, to each according to his ability. Then he went away. He who had received the five talents went at once and traded with them, and he made five talents more. So also he who had the two talents made two talents more. But he who had received the one talent went and dug in the ground and hid his master's money.

Now after a long time the master of those servants came and settled accounts with them. And he who had received the five talents came forward, bringing five talents more, saying, "Master, you delivered to me five talents; here I have made five talents more."

His master said to him, "Well done, good and faithful servant. You have been faithful over a little; I will set you over much. Enter into the joy of your master."

And he also who had the two talents came forward, saying, "Master, you delivered to me two talents; here I have made two talents more."

His master said to him, "Well done, good and faithful servant. You have been faithful over a little; I will set you over much. Enter into the joy of your master."

He also who had received the one talent came forward, saying, "Master, I knew you to be a hard man, reaping where you did not sow, and gathering where you scattered no seed, so I was afraid, and I went and hid your talent in the ground. Here you have what is yours."

But his master answered him, "You wicked and slothful servant! You knew that I reap where I have not sown and gather where I scattered no seed? Then you ought to have invested my money with the bankers, and at my coming I should have received what was my own with interest. So take the talent from him and give it to him who has the ten talents. For to everyone who has will more be given, and he will have an abundance. But from the one who has not, even what he has will be taken away. And cast the worthless servant into the outer darkness. In that place there will be weeping and gnashing of teeth."

Writer's Block

Paul Church was dead (heart attack). Andrew Cafferty was dead (cancer). Daniel Godolphin, as far as I could tell, lived off the grid in Thailand. Rebecca Johnson did not respond to the e-mail I sent to a Hotmail account that may or may not have belonged to the Rebecca Johnson who'd once dated Frederick Langley. Of the seemingly useful Freddy remembrants, that left only Richard Anders. I struggled, however, to write him a note—I kept drafting and redrafting—chiefly because I wasn't sure what to ask him. First I had to do my homework.

The field of Langley studies was pretty sparse. Fair enough, given the author's output and his relatively lightweight reputation. I found scholarly essays here and there on his depiction of female characters; his use of the uncanny; "Lifetime Warranty" and what it signified. Also a few postmortem assessments of Langley's career published in literary magazines, including *The New Yorker* and *Harper's*. Before long I was deep in the weeds. There I came across a reference to a lecture delivered at the 1997 Modern Language Association conference titled "Why Did He Stop?" *He* meaning Langley; *Stop* meaning stop publishing. I wasn't surprised that I had unearthed exactly what I wanted. It was an axiom in academia that any question one could possibly have about a writer, someone else had asked before.

The author was Barrett Pippen, then an assistant professor at Indiana University, now a professor emeritus at Mueller College in Harrison, New York. There was no copy of the lecture available at the library or online. When I wrote to Professor Pippen asking to take a look, he responded with a sob story featuring a localized fire and a hard drive. But he invited me to pay him a visit.

Lucky for him, or me, I kept a black Volvo S60 in mint condition stowed a few blocks away. Close at hand, if usually out of mind; I used it rarely, hence the mint condition. It didn't make sense to drive it to, say, the English department, which wasn't far afield. Even for longer trips, it was generally more convenient to take a cab. Still, I thought monthly garage fees well worth the psychological comfort of knowing I had an escape pod in the event of a terrorist attack. Or if I had to interview a Frederick Langley expert in a town without a Metro-North stop. To avoid peckishness on the road, I packed Pop-Tarts in Saran Wrap.

Situated in Westchester County about fifty miles south of New Harbor, Harrison looked like a foreigner's fantasy of small-town America, with its quaint stone post office, well-kept cemetery dating back to the Revolution, and well-kempt all-white residents. Mueller College struck me, coming from sprawling and imposing Collegiate, as cute and restrained — all brown brick and boxy. In the middle of the circular campus was its tallest structure, the three-story student center. I found Pippen's office at two o'clock (geographically) and ten o'clock (literally) — right on time.

The professor sat in a black rolling chair behind a hard plastic desk that he'd positioned near the window and the humming radiator. Because Professor Pippen shared a last name with the 1990s basketball player, I'd thought he might prove an exception to Mueller's otherwise pallid palette, but there was no relation to Scottie and no resemblance to him either. Professor Pippen had soft white skin, white hair, thick white eyebrows, and brown eyes. A big white mouse, more or less.

Apparently my Pippen was German and his family name was a corruption of the more common Pippin. He told me this "by the way." He told me a great many things "by the way," grinning cheerfully, exposing his gold molars, obviously delighted to have an audience. I learned that *Barrett* meant "brave as a bear," that he'd recently turned seventy, that he'd moved to the United States from East Germany as an adolescent, that he'd spent twenty-five years in Bloomington, Indiana, that he'd found the people there welcoming but that he preferred Harrison because it was so close to Manhattan and its theater district, that he enjoyed the theater but not musicals, that his wife, now deceased, had loved musicals, especially Andrew Lloyd Webber musicals, which he considered pure dreck, which had caused more than a few arguments between them.

When Professor Pippen recalled that I'd come to visit for a purpose and that the purpose was to better understand Langley's career, his manner changed. He'd given me the impression that he was juggling topics like plates, letting one crash to the floor when he saw another he preferred. Langley, though, occupied the professor's attention. His old subject made him focus.

"You've read *Freddy Remembered?*" he asked, sounding suddenly like a villain in a World War II epic. His German accent was most prominent on *r*'s, which he rolled like tanks into Belgium.

"His friend Daniel Godolphin said it was weird that Langley stopped producing. I think so too."

"Is it possible he just decided he'd had enough?" I asked. "That he'd released good work and was satisfied with it? Omega, the last letter of the Greek alphabet, can mean 'conclusion' or 'end.' Maybe the title of his last collection was an announcement."

I felt good about that etymological insight, which had come to me in a flash—like in those stories of inspiration that I had never trusted.

"That is a truly ridiculous theory. It sounds like something Langley would have told people to justify his lack of energy. He was twenty-six when he wrote *Omega*! No one is satisfied so young."

"So illuminate me."

"Frederick Langley developed a nasty case of writer's block."

"That's it?"

"Writer's block may be more interesting than you think. Creative inhibition is certainly a symptom of an underlying disease," he said, evoking another German stereotype, not the military commander but the good doctor.

If an author stops producing, according to Professor Pippen, it's often because he perceives a gap between his abilities and his reputation. Picture a writer who toils away in obscurity to create his first work. He doesn't know if he'll make it in the literary world or even find a publisher. But he does and, lo and behold, he's a success. When the author—because he's an author now, not just a writer—sits down to begin his second book, he's paralyzed with anxiety. What if it's not as good as the first? What if the critics tear it apart? Now that he has something to lose, he can't put words on the page.

Moving from the generic to the specific, Professor Pippen examined the case of Joseph Mitchell, the *New Yorker* writer. Mitchell joined the magazine in 1938 and wrote several classic pieces, chief among them "Joe Gould's Secret" in 1964. That was the last story he ever published. When Mitchell died, in 1996, Calvin Trillin quipped that he "was writing away at a normal pace until some professor called him the greatest living master of the English declarative sentence and stopped him cold." Although Trillin was just repeating gossip, Professor Pippen asserted that he was probably right: Mitchell couldn't handle his success.

Coming back around to Langley, the professor noted that, as a young man, he'd found writing easy, and according to his college editor Paul Church, he'd barely revised. More than that, writing was almost a compulsion. He left a party to write "Lifetime Warranty" in a single night. But after *Omega*—nothing. When he went to Europe, he didn't even bring along his typewriter. Surely the timing wasn't a coincidence. Surely, like Mitchell, "critical warmth stopped Langley cold." That must have been devastating psychologically. Truly, it must have been excruciating for Langley to find he could no longer produce—an argument that also handily explained why Langley spent the last years of his life "not far from here, or from New Harbor" in "the silent obscurity of his brother's Connecticut attic." (Apparently that was public knowledge.) He was a broken man.

I felt I had to share my intelligence.

"Professor Pippen," I said, "were you aware that Langley kept notebooks in that Connecticut attic?" He brought together his bushy eyebrows. No, he wasn't aware. "I'm not sure what he was writing. Apparently story ideas and a draft of something longer. The Elston bought his notebooks in an estate sale, but they're not public."

"Why?"

"It may not have the legal rights to them. There's a lawsuit."

"Collegiate will win in the end. It has too much money to lose."

I couldn't read the professor's expression: happy or wistful or nostalgic or a bit of all three. He stared out his window to a wide lawn crisscrossed with stone pathways.

"Anna, this is terrible," he said, his voice full of melodrama. "You've made me feel ambitious. I almost want to study Langley again."

"You could do that."

"Yes, I could. But why should I? I'm emeritus. My job is to sit here looking distinguished."

"Then — because you enjoy research."

"I detest research."

"I see. You're more teacher than researcher."

"Not at all. I detest teaching too."

"What do you like?"

"Reading," he rolled.

My heart beat quicker and sweat gathered in my armpits, not only because I'd been scared into thinking I'd created a competitor but also because I'd met a kindred spirit. I knew, and had admitted to myself, that I did not enjoy teaching or grading. I did not have the generosity of spirit necessary to take pleasure in bringing other people along. I also knew that I found research frustrating and that my mind wandered at the library or wherever else I tried to work. On the few occasions I'd published papers, however, I'd found that gratifying. Arguably I liked having researched, not actually doing research. The life of a professor emerita seemed ideal: work behind me, sitting around ahead, as close to a permanent state of cultured leisure we modern Americans could hope to get, aristocratic dabbling having fallen out of vogue. (One obvious difference was that professors earned their lassitude whereas aristocrats were entitled to it.)

"You must think the notebooks invalidate my writer's-block argument," Professor Pippen said after a while.

"Maybe he had it and then overcame it," I said. "But it's true that neither theory we've discussed leads easily to Langley's last-gasp productivity. If he stopped intentionally, what made him change his mind? If he had writer's block, how did he get past it?"

Fieldwork

A map proved Professor Pippen right: Milford lay roughly three-quarters of the way between my present location and my destination. *Not far from here or from New Harbor.* A professor emerita would not have bothered, but I wasn't there yet, obviously. Two appointments in one day—a strong rebuttal to allegations of laziness, and I hadn't so much as opened a Word document.

The online People Finder service cost $9.99. Family name: Langley. First name: Thomas. State: Connecticut. City: Milford. His last known address was 2514 Matthew Street. I took I-95, an unpleasant road scarred with potholes from decades of low-tax political campaigns. Cars jostled for position on the highway like blocks in a game of Tetris governed by the chaos theory. Everything would fit together nicely if only the SUV switched places with the Saab. I took the Boston Post Road exit and then Wheelers Farms Road, which cut through Milford, connecting I-95 to the Wilbur Cross Parkway.

At around twelve thirty I passed the usual suburban fare: a low-rise office building surrounded by a large parking lot, a depressing playground featuring a single rickety swing set. The metal and rubber swings jiggled in the breeze. Farther from the highway:

wooden houses, satellite dishes on shingled roofs, neat front lawns, and two-car garages.

Helen had grown up in a tasteful white Colonial with green shutters. It was much nicer than the run-down bungalow near Worcester Square, and the gap between the two made me feel sorry for her. She had come down in the world. Now she had little choice but to accept checks from PhD candidates.

The current occupant was pruning his hedges with two-handed shears. When he turned to face me, he failed to close them. It looked as though he were warding me off, threatening me with his blades: a horror-movie sentry. Preposterously, I had neither planned in advance what I would say to the owner nor integrated a third party into my mental projection of the visit. (The first party was I; the second was the house.) It wasn't too late to pretend I'd turned down the wrong driveway.

"Hi," I said, charging ahead. "My name's Anna Brisker. I'm a graduate student at Collegiate University."

Still the man kept hold of his gaping shears, precluding a handshake. He was roughly Helen's age, with a sturdy chest and shoulders. But starting at the hips, his flesh loosened most unfortunately, descending into fat, round, womanly thighs. His upper half sat on his lower half like a man on a horse—one with flabby hindquarters. Body type: aging centaur. As for his face, he had a wan, dissipated look common among redheads past their prime, with beady brown eyes that gave him a sinister cast, exacerbated by the clippers.

"I study Frederick Langley, the famous author," I continued. "You probably don't know it, but he used to live here."

"I do know it," said the man. "He was my mother's co-brother-in-law."

"Pardon?"

"My mother's sister, Edith, was married to Freddy's brother, Thomas."

"Wonderful," I improvised, still puzzled by the relationship, not to mention how he'd come into possession of the house. "Maybe I can interview you."

"I wasn't close with Freddy, actually."

"That's too bad."

"But you didn't come to see me. So what are you doing here?"

What indeed. I explained that I wanted to see the house for research, or fieldwork, claiming that academics often paid such visits to add color to their scholarly writing. (I left out my less tangible motives.)

Helen's cousin was not inclined to grant my wish. Ian, as he instructed me to call him, said that he'd repainted since his aunt and uncle had died and that he'd bought new furniture. He also said he had a great deal of clipping ahead of him. But I countered that paint color mattered less than the space itself and that he wouldn't need to take much time away from his chores — or any, really, if he let me show myself around. If only to prevent this more dramatic option, which seemed to shock him, Ian relented.

Remembering Moses and Pharaoh, I barged ahead before Ian could change his mind, speed-walking straight through a bare foyer into a large sitting room with a fireplace. It was dark despite the fact that the room was lined with windows. The hedges blocked the light. There, Ian grudgingly accepted his obligations as a host.

Ian showed me the kitchen, where I knew Helen's maid had served her hot chocolate, and the home office, where Ian kept the serious hardcover books he wanted people to think he'd read.

There was a mudroom in the rear with a view of the backyard, just as orderly as the front. My restroom break taught me that Ian enjoyed lavender-scented cleaning supplies and that he shopped at Costco; the bathroom closet was stuffed with toilet paper, lavender hand soap, lavender body soap, lavender shampoo, lavender conditioner. Enough to get through the first year of the Apocalypse smelling of relaxation.

Next, Ian led me upstairs, breathing heavily with every step. In a perfunctory manner he opened each door off a central hallway that was padded in thick, beige carpeting. Helen hadn't given me enough information to guess which was her childhood room and which the guest room. The master was obvious. (It was the only one large enough to fit a king-size bed.) Ian had set up shop there. Back to the hallway. What I'd assumed was a closet door concealed a narrow staircase that brought us at last to what I was after: the attic.

"Would you mind if I went alone? I'll only be a minute."

Ian let me have my way, perhaps because he was still out of breath. He was in such poor shape that he couldn't handle moving his tongue and legs at the same time. Below the ribs lurked heavy cargo.

So this was it. Old furniture, trash bags, cleaning supplies. Without all the flotsam, it could have been fairly nice. The walls were whitewashed and skylights let in plenty of sun. It was quiet, private, and well ventilated. Still, it was difficult to imagine some- one living there — unless that someone was a Victorian hysteric with a tyrannical husband.

Where the ceiling slanted downward, the skylight exposed a view of the neighboring house. It needed new shingles. How many times had Langley looked out on that rooftop? It would have been in better condition then. Or might have been. Enough time had passed between his death and the present moment for two or even three repair cycles. I sat down on the dusty floor with my back against the wall. I recognized that I was waiting for something to happen to me, internally — something that would reveal to me Langley's state of mind post-*Omega* and post-Europe. That was the true purpose of my fieldwork.

One summer during college I'd traveled to England with my family. My father had insisted on seeing Chartwell, Winston Churchill's country house, so that he could meander through the rooms where the wartime prime minister had entertained politicians and written consequential letters. He'd conceded that he probably wouldn't learn anything substantial about Churchill or Nazi resistance by touching the dead man's floorboards, but he had said he wanted to get a "sense" of the place.

At the time I'd felt superior to my father. He seemed to have succumbed to a cheap, modern animism fostered by the tourism-industrial complex. Now it was my turn to want a "sense" of a place. The house, however, was just a house, and the attic was just an attic. It had no aura. Langley felt far away and inscrutable. The author had left no metaphysical trace, or it was inaccessible to me. Cohabiting with Langley in space but not time would tell me nothing.

Several cardboard boxes were piled up in a dark corner. I knew it was wrong to look through them but I wanted to anyway; that which a person stows away — does not throw away but does not keep in use — can provide just as much intelligence as medical records and tax returns. Or so I told myself.

Actually, as I rifled through them one by one, I found tchotchkes and stuffed animals that revealed nothing, and a smooth black stone, probably culled from a sentimental walk on the beach, that appealed to me for some reason. I pocketed it, barely conscious of the theft, feeling there was no harm in it. *Is a rock private property?* I wondered. *Are rocks ownable?* Yes, actually; they were the first owned things. *I own these rocks. Don't stand on them.*

A minute later I came across a bit of paper folded over several times into a tough square. I smoothed it out. There was writing on both sides that did not at all resemble the penmanship I'd seen on the *Qui transtulit sustinet* postcard. It was neater, tighter. It must have been a fragment of a longer work because it started midthought:

not pretty. She had wild curly brown hair not typically to my liking and thick ankles. Her stomach fat bubbled over her tight yet unfashionable skirts. Women should never wear tweed, I'm sure you'd agree. Yet there was something about her. That fat belly transfixed me. Jiggling and quivering, it hypnotized me, like the white dotted line on the highway. Do you see what I mean?

Patients, as I'm sure I've told you, as a matter of routine fantasize that we think of them once they've left the office, as they think of us. Generally this is not the case but to my shame I did think of Bianca, and did so often. All her petty hopes and complaints caught and held my attention. Would her boss ask her again to fetch his coffee? Would he complain if the coffee wasn't hot enough? If it was too hot? Would her sister cruelly flaunt her fertility? I looked forward to her arrival with the intensity of a boy in love for the first time. Was I? In love, that is.

We call what happens between a psychiatrist and a patient transference. That is to say, we attribute the feelings between psychiatrist and patient to transference. If she felt angry with me, surely she was venting her aggression toward her father etc. etc. etc., and if she was fond of me she was trying to recapture the feeling of a father's unquestioning love etc. etc. etc. And I would play the good father and the bad father etc. etc. etc. But transference also occurs outside of this relationship, outside of an office setting, and we do not doubt that there can be transference *and* love. Perhaps what we had was transference *and* love. I did act on my feelings, repeatedly.

You could not believe I could have feelings of this sort. Now you know I can. I do. The mistake you make and have made since childhood is to assume absurdly that I do not feel what I do not say. I am a blind spot for you. I make you forget your sophistication. You think what I do not discuss does not exist for me. This from a man who told me once to ask myself when reading novels what was missing to understand what was there. What's not in *Middlemarch*? I couldn't begin to answer. Food and drink, you said. How delightful I found that observation. Do me the credit of believing I am at least as complicated as an old book, or you.

That was all. I didn't know who'd written the confession. Thomas Langley? He was a psychiatrist. And I didn't know the identity of the intended recipient. Frederick Langley? I dimly recalled an academic paper titled "What's Not in *Middlemarch*." Had the correspondent read it, or anticipated it? But I didn't know when the paper had been published. It dawned on me that I didn't even know who'd packed the boxes. Not Langley. Anyway, the Salvation Army had taken everything after his funeral. I stood up, knees creaking as I extended my legs. The sound transported me through the years to the moment when I'd know with excruciating certainty that I'd never again walk without pain.

First the rhomboids, then the knees.

Ian's heaving announced his approach. He entered timidly, as if he were the intruder and not I. Or maybe his waddle made him seem timid when in reality he felt bold. I was grateful he hadn't found me kneeling on the floor, examining his possessions. Nevertheless, I must have looked weird to him, just standing in his attic. Perhaps he regretted letting me explore unsupervised. I'd said I was a graduate student at Collegiate, which was a way of indicating that I was a responsible, upright sort of person, but he hadn't asked for identification. Perhaps he thought I was a grifter. If he demanded that I turn out my pockets, he'd find the black stone.

"Has this visit been helpful? To your research?"

"Immensely. Thank you."

"What aspect of Freddy's work do you study, exactly?"

"His late-career disposition," I blurted out.

Ian seemed to accept that description, vague and confusing though it was. He didn't really give a damn what I studied. And that was natural. Outside of the parent-child relationship or the rare healthy romantic relationship, people generally did not care how others occupied themselves. Other people's lives were interesting mainly on the level of trivia or collectorship. *He's a zoologist, isn't that strange?* Or *I know one detective, two filmmakers, and three lawyers.*

"Even Freddy's late career was over before I knew him."

"Ah," I said, trying to sound like a crusty scholar, encrusted with a knowing wisdom.

"When I met him, I remember thinking to myself: *This guy wrote books?* I couldn't line up Freddy's past as an artist with the man who lived up here. I couldn't picture him crafting delicate stories about fishing trips. He wasn't — put together."

"Artists often aren't."

"Yeah, all right. What you expect isn't always what you get. I hear all the famous actors are short and Tom Cruise is tiny. But everyone said Freddy changed a lot. He was sullen and he drank too much. I guess he was depressed. You know the story, if you study Freddy. Should I show you out?"

It wasn't a subtle offer, but he'd made it politely.

"You must live in *New* Harbor. New *Harb*or, I mean." At first, Ian had said the city's name like a tourist, *New* Harbor, then corrected himself and stressed the second syllable, New *Harb*or. "It's not as terrible as it once was, is it? You missed the worst of it, the really grisly stuff: the arson-for-insurance scheme and the carjacking spree. The city was on fire."

We arrived at the entrance. I couldn't wait any longer.

"I should have said, earlier, that I know your cousin Helen Langley."

"How?" Ian asked, frowning.

"She's helping me with my work, but I didn't tell her I was coming by. If you mention my visit to her —"

"Unlikely. We're not on speaking terms. Here's some free advice: Don't hang around Helen."

"She's been very nice, very generous with her time."

"Listen, you can find the basics[2] in a trashy *Town and Country* story from a while ago. I guess they thought the family drama would play well with their more culturally inclined readers."

---

2   The basics:

1981: Frederick Langley dies young, leaving no will. Frederick's closest living blood relative, Thomas Langley, automatically inherits the entire estate under Connecticut intestacy law.

1982: Thomas decides to formally split estate proceeds with his daughter, Helen Langley.

1984: Helen announces that she's moving to Italy instead of finishing college and will subsist for a time on her inheritance.

1986: Helen returns home in need of money.

1987: Helen leaves home, taking with her Thomas's entire Frederick Langley collection.

1988: Thomas discovers his German and French editions of *Brutality and Delicacy* at a rare-book store in New York.

1992: Helen is accused of defrauding a client who paid her to track down a first printing of Henry VanderMeer's *Life in the Cage*. Thomas pays his daughter's legal bills.

1994: Helen is found guilty and sentenced to community service.

1995: On the basis of Helen's conviction, Thomas succeeds in wresting back full control of the Frederick Langley estate.

2002: Edith Langley dies.

2004: Thomas dies. In his will, he turns over Frederick Langley's estate, including control of Frederick Langley's copyright, to Frederick Langley's publisher, Finer and Bloch. Thomas leaves his money to charity and his house to Edith's nephew Ian.

The Notebook

"What's a *sticking-place*?" Helen asked. She was reading *Macbeth*.

> MACBETH: If we should fail?
> LADY MACBETH: We fail!
> But screw your courage to the sticking-place, and
>   we'll not fail.

I said: "I don't think it means anything specific. If I'd written that instead of the greatest literary genius of all time, everyone would've said it was a bad description. Too general. What comes to mind when you read *sticking-place?* Nothing. You get no visual. At best, the spot on the underside of your school desk where you stow your gum."

Jeez, this kid takes sloppy notes. Doodles, mostly, and just one gem. The editors of the First Folio said of Shakespeare: "His mind and hand went together: And what he thought he uttered with that easiness that we have scarce received from him a blot in his papers."

Shake'n Bake. I was like that, at first. Yes, not now, but at first. I won't say I achieved even sticking-place-level prose. But I was like that. Easy-peasy lemon squeezy. Not a blot, not a messy pink eraser trace. All the struggle happened before the words ever hit the page.

A story in which every single sentence contains at least one cliché. If not absolutely every sentence, then as often as possible.

"I'm nervous as a cat on a hot tin roof," said Dick.

"Screw your courage to the sticking-place," Jane replied.

"Leave it to my better half to add salt to the wound."

"What doesn't kill you makes you stronger."

What's the difference between a cliché and a saying? Richard would know. Scratch that nonsense. He would pretend to know and make something up. He did not know how to say, "I don't know." Just could not get those words out of his mouth. A critic once slammed a passage in "Look Over There" in which I used the word *inveigle* when, he said, I must have wanted *finagle*. The critic was right. Richard tried to comfort me: "There is nothing worse than a young critic." (How did he know the critic's age?) I said: "Isn't it your job to catch things like that?" He said: "I thought it was intentional." (Impossible.) He was as ignorant as I of the true meaning of those words. The other possibility was that he had never even bothered to read "Look Over There." Which was worse, ignorance or apathy? Richard did not love "Lifetime Warranty" but I know I'll never write anything so good again, it was my peak, my high point, my crowning achievement. All the critics, including the young critic, agreed.

Helen said her allowance was too small. I said "Yup, I can believe that." I said: "Your father is a stingy fella. Sorry to break it to ya." I didn't have any cash handy so I signed and inscribed a first printing of *Brutality and Delicacy* and told her to sell it. Anyway, it's not the only copy around here. After some back-and-forth she agreed. She reported that the buyer at the used-book store looked like Statler the Muppet, smelled like brussels sprouts, and gave her $175. Not bad! Helen offered to split her winnings but I told her not to worry. "Tomorrow in the shopping mall think on me," I said. She did not get the joke. She is not a good student. She'd rather go out with her friends than study.

> Books! 'tis a dull and endless strife:
> Come, hear the woodland linnet,
> How sweet his music! on my life,
> There's more of wisdom in it.

I should tell Helen about the slothful servant. From the one who has not, even what she has will be taken away. It shouldn't be that way. But it is. Idle! Hands! Helen! Americans would not empathize with the third servant. No, not at all. Reap what you sow is the ethos of this great land stretching from sea to shining sea. Milton made the obvious leap from talent as coin to talent as natural ability.

> *When I consider how my light is spent,*
> *Ere half my days, in this dark world and wide,*
> *And that one talent which is death to hide*
> *Lodged with me useless, though my soul more bent*
>
> *To serve therewith my Maker, and present*
> *My true account, lest He, returning, chide;*
> *"Doth God exact day-labour, light denied?"*
> *I fondly ask.*

"Love is patient. Love is kind. Love does not envy," said the new throw pillow. "Have faith," replied the usurped throw pillow, decrepit from use, destined for an odorous afterlife in the dingy doghouse.

"Good morning, sunshine," Dick said.

"It's raining cats and dogs," Jane replied. "And when it rains, it pours."

"Look at the bright side, will you, dearest?"

"I am not one to see the glass half full, Dick, you know that."

"Jane, I cannot help but look at the world through rose-colored glasses."

"And I cannot lighten up no matter how hard I try."

I'll set "Dick and Jane" in Concord but I won't call it Concord. It'll be obvious to anyone familiar with the place. But I don't want the burden of capturing it. And the veil of fiction will force the reader to acknowledge the author. Me, me, me!

Cemetery Picnic

As anticipated, the University of Chicago offered Evan a tenure-track position. Evelyn, attached to her fiancé like a tapeworm to an intestine, was negotiating an adjunct job at the same university. Everyone was very happy for them. They deserved it, as Professor Davidoff put it. At least Chicago had more going for it than New Harbor, even if it wasn't New York, as I put it.

To celebrate, Evan and Evelyn insisted I join them for a picnic at Vine Street Cemetery, an unpleasant tradition dating back to our first year of graduate school. A classmate from Southern California had complained one too many times about the quality of life on the East Coast, where winters were so cold that we all spent our days huddled indoors. He missed hiking and strolling on the beach. He missed fresh air. As a taunt, we'd planned an outdoor lunch. We'd selected the cemetery because it was more private than any of the lawns on the campus proper and also because it was more conducive to jokes about contracting a fatal case of tuberculosis, that most literary disease.

Although we'd all had a terrible time, the picnic had become an annual event. Of course, over the years, the picnic crowd had shrunk as more and more of us had left New Harbor until, on this occasion, only the three of us were available. That was not, in my opinion, a quorum, and I was surprised the loving couple wanted the pleasure of my company. Nevertheless, I went along.

Evelyn brought thermoses full of hot toddies, two baguettes, a wheel of Brie, fruit salad, plastic plates, plastic cutlery, and napkins. I brought Hershey's milk chocolate bars, which the others mocked as lowbrow until they wanted to eat them. Evan brought nothing, though he took partial credit for Evelyn's largesse. We spread a tarp and blankets neatly over a renowned industrialist's grave and raised our thermoses to honor Evan's good fortune.

"Gird your loins!" said Evan.

We drank.

Evelyn situated herself between Evan's legs and leaned back into his chest. He kissed her temple and wrapped his arms around her, a warmhearted gesture that made me feel the cold and think of Helen, my new friend, if I could call her that, now lost, a victim of her past. Forced to rely only on myself, I embraced my knees as Evan had embraced Evelyn and thought, not for the first time, that I would never see Helen again. Should never see her again. Should never see such a person again.

She was a thief—and a vulture. A vulture who'd lived for a time off her uncle's remains. Despite that, I felt sorry to lose her. She was more interesting than Evan or Evelyn; her house was more comfortable than New Campus Library; the meal she'd prepared for me was the only proper one I'd eaten in months. Faint praise, but I was fond of her. Plus, she was useful to me. I was fond of her, but I was wrong to feel fond of her. She was useful to me, but I could manage without her. Round and round I went. Assuming the *Town and Country* story was true, I had no out. There was no alternative but to pursue Frederick Langley without Helen Langley. And what grounds did I have to doubt the story? None at all. I had to renounce her. Anything less was unreasonable. I should never see her again. I would never see her again.

"Gird your loins!" Evan said once more.

We drank again. I felt unsure how to behave: Young and ebullient or old and civilized? One of the problems with graduate school, generally, was that we didn't have an obvious model for what a good time should look like. Manhattan intellectuals could ape Woody Allen or, in a pinch, Noah Baumbach; professors had Edward Albee; undergraduates could choose from any number of Hollywood blockbusters. (Freshmen hung posters of John Belushi in *Animal House* above their beds.) We doctoral candidates were left more at sea, which was to say, more at liberty to create our own version of fun, and left at liberty, we floundered.

"How does one gird one's loins?" I asked.

"It's just Evan's clever way of saying 'cheers,'" said Evelyn.

"Right," I said. "I'm asking what it means literally."

This was how we spoke to one another.

Evan, delighted to find his expertise in demand, explained that *loins* could mean the area between one's hips and ribs. One could gird one's loins by wrapping a belt around one's waist. Unable to resist the opportunity to flaunt his extensive knowledge of Milton, Evan also informed us that in *Paradise Lost,* after the fall, Adam tells Eve that they should gird their loins with leaves, meaning they should tie leaves around their hips.

Later I looked up the passage.

> *O might I here*
> *In solitude live savage, in some glade*

Obscured where highest woods, impenetrable
To star or sunlight, spread their umbrage broad,
And brown as evening: cover me ye pines,
Ye cedars, with innumerable boughs
Hide me where I may never see them more.
But let us now, as in bad plight, devise
What best may for the present serve to hide
The parts of each from other that seem most
To shame obnoxious and unseemliest seen,
Some tree whose broad smooth leaves, together sewed,
And girded on our loins, may cover round
Those middle parts that this newcomer, shame,
There sit not and reproach us as unclean.

The invention of clothing and shame and secret-keeping. And the notion that some things are better left concealed.

"Is *Paradise Lost* worthwhile?" I asked.

"You haven't read it?" asked Evelyn.

"Missed it somehow."

"That's the ultimate Humiliation trump card," said Evan, referring to a literary parlor game in which participants accrue points for classic texts that they've never read. It played a pivotal role in David Lodge's campus novel *Changing Places*, as my classmates likely knew. We were suckers for books about academics.

"Should we play a round?" asked Evelyn.

"God, no," I said. "That never ends well."

These were not people but characters—lousy caricatures. If,

contrary to appearances, they had depths, they were invisible to me, because we interacted as graduate students, not as human beings. Evelyn, the hanger-on. Evan, the Stakhanovite. He churned out research while I waited for my toaster to hurry up and spit out my breakfast. Yet I knew he lacked the spark that separated great scholarly minds from the merely successful.

"I heard a rumor," Evan said, "that undergrads like to have sex on this grave. It's a sort of competition, part of a frat initiation."

Would the industrialist's spirit prefer to host inept undergraduate copulation or inane graduate-level conversation?

"Actually," said Evan, "I might be thinking of another grave, a lexicographer's grave."

A lexicographer, I felt sure, would choose inept copulation. I would too. I hadn't copulated with an undergraduate since I was an undergraduate. (In fact, I probably hadn't even touched one in years, not since the last class I'd had the misfortune to TA, back before I'd fulfilled my teaching requirements.) Inane graduate chatter, conversely, was as familiar as tinnitus. Thinking back to the era before that buzzing sound had asserted itself was like trying to imagine my body before puberty; I knew I had once gone about the world without breasts, but the sense memory was gone. A mixed and mangled metaphor, but it worked well enough.

Evelyn nattered — I didn't listen to a thing she said, really could not have repeated a word of her multi-minute speech, though *Evan* and *Chicago* were safe bets. In time, numb with cold and heavy with cheese, we resorted to career gossip, which in our case meant rehearsing facts we already knew. Listing gave us communal pleasure.

Of the seven people who'd started the PhD program together, one — the Californian — had dropped out quickly. No one had heard from him again. Another had found a job at the University of Michigan after five years, but he was the son of a Michigan professor and it was easy to dismiss his achievement as the product of nepotism. There was no comparably convenient explanation for why a third had finished in six years and secured a postdoctoral fellowship in the United Kingdom. Evan and Evelyn were bound for Chicago. Our last classmate, who commuted from Brooklyn and rarely stuck around to socialize — hence his absence now — had interviews lined up at colleges in North Carolina, Indiana, and Pennsylvania.

If the Brooklyn commuter prevailed, only I would be left. I, of all people. I, who, if PhD programs had yearbooks, would once have been voted Most Likely to Succeed. Professor Davidoff had been so proud of me, once. My family so impressed, once. The distance between what I had been once and what I was now hit me with the force of a scientific discovery. Or an illness. It was creeping from my brain to my bowels, quite like the tequila the last time I'd seen this cloying couple, when Evelyn said: "I thought I should mention, I might not go after that adjunct job."

"Really? Why not?"

"I just think it might be time to do something else."

I'd heard that Evelyn's dissertation on Jane Austen wasn't going well — that it read like a book report. Still, I was taken aback.

"I've loved these past few years, but I don't think I'm cut out for academia," said Evelyn.

She said she didn't care about the things that other academics considered important and did care about the things that they found childish. She got wrapped up in novels, getting attached to characters as if they were real people. When she'd told her adviser that she had a crush on Darcy — the *Pride and Prejudice* character — the adviser had responded that she was "cute about fiction," as in not serious enough to concentrate on linguistic style or structure. Although Evelyn had tried, for a while, to break her bad habits and approach literature more dispassionately, she'd realized eventually that she did not want to change.

I found this all remarkably on point. Graduate school wasn't for people who loved Darcy, or any other literary creation, because academia wasn't about love of literature. It was about extracting arguments from texts. And *Darcy is dreamy* didn't count. "Save your feelings for your Sunday book club" was how Professor Davidoff had put it in a seminar long ago.

Evelyn concluded: "I'm looking forward to reading just for fun."

"I think I lost that ability a long time ago," I said. "You, Evan?"

"Pretty much. I do enjoy figuring things out, though. That moment when an argument falls into place or, short of that, when you realize you're going in the right direction."

"You're in hot pursuit."

"Yes."

"Your quarry's in sight. You draw your weapon. Soon you'll throw your author in a bag, cook him, and feast on his flesh. I know what you mean. Recently I heard that the Elston's holding on to a couple of notebooks that belonged to Frederick Langley —" Evan and Evelyn turned to look at each other. "What is it?"

"He's my time period," said Evan. "I was telling Evelyn recently that I should at least mention him when I turn my dissertation into a book. His stories fit the theme too: moments of enlightenment. But I didn't know his notebooks were on campus."

"Weird. I feel hungry again," I said, desperate to end the conversation, not that it had really begun. I didn't want Evan on my trail.

"They're at the Elston, you said?"

"I shouldn't have mentioned it."

"Why not?"

"It's complicated."

"Who can tell me more, then?"

I tore a hefty wedge from the last baguette and reached for the Brie. There was a girl at my high school named Brie, same spelling. During my family vacation in England, I ordered a baguette with Brie and cranberry sauce almost every day for lunch. (I gained a not insignificant amount of weight.) In a taste test I had not been able to differentiate Brie from Camembert. In *Twin Peaks,* Jerry Horne brought Brie and butter sandwiches back from France. He and his brother, Ben, ate them lustily as they planned their crimes.

Evan and Evelyn revived a conversation they'd been having for days about Chicago real estate. It was a sellers' market, said Evan. And yet, it was better to own than rent, he said, playing devil's advocate. Besides, Hyde Park had a captive population. Across the country thousands of couples were having the same discussion using the same words. As for me: I looked toward the massive stone columns that marked the entrance to the cemetery, avoiding eye contact until I could think of a neutral topic. Such things came easier to other people.

Dreamwork

Outside, a homeless man (presumably a homeless man) directed a stream of obscenities at a hapless undergraduate (presumably a hapless undergraduate) who had dared to cross his path. I did not see the encounter but I heard it from my second-story bedroom twenty-five feet above the street — heard enough to presume. I'd left a window open to combat my fever. The argument finally ended after the undergraduate said, "Here! Here!" These words, I gathered, accompanied a significant charitable contribution.

The cemetery picnic had destroyed my immune system. I could do nothing but sleep, cough, and swallow Tylenol. As if that wasn't enough to prove that I was truly sick, I found I could take no pleasure in the fact that work was out of the question. Words blurred together on the page; it was like trying to read in a dream.

Too weak to carry my dirty sheets down to the basement laundry room, I felt (and was) surrounded by germs. I also felt (and was) quite alone. Except for the germs. Professor Davidoff was in loco parentis, but it obviously wasn't appropriate for me to request his attention. Evelyn answered the phone when I called, but, suddenly ashamed, I hung up.

What's up? she texted.

Pocket-dial, I responded.

There was one other person I didn't think it right to try.

"Did you hear the one about the American banker and the Mexican fisherman?" the homeless man shouted. "The fisherman goes out on his boat a couple hours a day. The banker says, Why don't you stay out longer? The fisherman says, I catch enough to eat. The banker says, If you catch more than you need, you can start a business. The fisherman says, Then what? The banker says, Then you make money. The fisherman says, Then what? The banker says, Then you make more money. The fisherman says, Then what? The banker says, Then you retire. The fisherman says, Then what? The banker says, Then all you have to do is go out on your boat a couple hours a day."

A passerby must have said something because the homeless man paused.

"I saw that on a Jimmy John's sandwich wrapper," he resumed.

I wavered in and out of consciousness. Delirious. Because I felt too weak to seek out the couch in front of the television, I had nothing but my clock radio for entertainment. Sam Cooke. Either the song or the old-timey-ness of listening to the radio in a darkened room made me nostalgic for an America I'd never known. The colorful skirts and ponytails and drive-ins and heavy cars and institutional racism that at least no one could deny. The summer evenings spent worrying about Russians and typing class and boys named Bob, Dick, Harry, John, Freddy. I stared sightlessly at the ceiling, remembering nights spent staring sightlessly at the ceiling. Nights full of dread. Nights before exams, like that history test on the Great Depression. All those acronyms that blurred together: AAA,

CCC, WPA, FHA, FERA, FSA. Static on the radio. Behind it, Merle Haggard. One and only rebel child. Toward the bad he kept on turning, till his mother couldn't hold him anymore.

My mother used to read to me at bedtime, mostly stories from the Torah and from classical antiquity that some clever editor had cut and marketed to children. Because she thought it was important to cultivate my imagination, she'd shrug when I asked for her adult, authoritative judgment.

"Would Abraham really have sacrificed Isaac?"

"What do you think?"

"Was Odysseus right to kill the suitors, after he'd stayed away so long?"

"What do you think?"

In the 1970s, the academy embraced the theory that texts weren't finished until they had an audience; the reader was an active agent who imparted "real existence" to the work, conferring meaning through interpretation. All the author did was write the words; the reader brought them to life. Literature, then, was a performing art, and as a child I had learned how to play my part rather than depend on my mother to do it for me. If a tree falls in the forest but doesn't make a sound. Same concept. If a homeless man waits on the street for a passerby but no one passes by. Same concept.

A cool, pleasant night. When the homeless man chases me I can't move my legs. My shoes stick to the concrete. My muscles fail to obey even the simplest commands. But I get away from him somehow to meet Helen on the green. How I'd missed her, her presence, how I behaved in her presence. I was an object at rest, staying at rest until I'd felt the influence of her unbalanced force. In her absence I worried inertia would take over again. She leads me inside the Episcopal church, sits me down in a pew, and points to a black briefcase. Inside it I see Langley's notebooks. Eagerly I flip through them but I can't make out the words. Each time I try to seize upon a sentence, it dissolves into squiggles. Helen lights a purple cigarette with a gold filter.

"You can't do that in here," I say.

She tosses the cigarette in the briefcase. Immediately the notebooks catch fire. Purple and gold flames shoot upward.

"What have you done?" I ask, the burning briefcase on my lap.

"Only what he wanted," she responds.

I run outside the church and ask a stranger for water. He gives me a six-pack of Evian. I run back inside and pour one bottle after another into the briefcase. The fire goes out but it's too late. The notebooks have been reduced to ash.

"Did that just happen?"

"What do you think?"

The Notebook

Some mornings are meant for doing nothing. Some afternoons are meant for doing nothing. Some evenings are meant for doing nothing. Some days are meant for doing nothing. Some weeks are meant for doing nothing. Some months are meant for doing nothing. Some years are meant for doing nothing. Some lifetimes are meant for doing nothing. Nothing: the antidote to boredom. Nothing: the only pure pleasure. A perfect day for nothing, no one seems to say.

I can't remember the title of that book. Someone's name. I didn't appreciate it when I read it but it stuck with me. Slow and steady and wise. The man refuses to get out of bed for the first fifty pages—at which point he walks to a chair and sits down. So it goes on and on, more or less uninterrupted. All the tension in the novel comes from the man's passivity in the face of the world's demand for activity.

Dad was at his most dramatic when he went into his idle-hands riff. Up at the lectern, eyebrows arched, he'd show the students his hands, look at the students, look at his hands as if they were foreign objects rising before him through some otherworldly power. "Idle! Hands! Are! The devil's! Workshop! Workshops! Keep! Away! The devil!" I was never sure whether he really believed in God or not but, my, did he like all the accoutrements. The Protestant work-ethic aesthetic. It was all so long ago, so many decades. I'm old now, ought to just get over it. But childhood stays with you. Living with Thomas makes it fresh again.

A woman wakes up in the morning and turns off her alarm clock. Still in bed, Katherine Smith plans out what she will wear and what she will eat for breakfast. She thinks about how she will commute to work, who she will see, what she will say to them, how she will feel about what she says and does, how other people will feel about what she says and does. Finally Katherine considers what she will eat for dinner and whether she will allow herself dessert and imagines what she will read before sleep. At the end of the story she tells herself that she really should get out of bed already, what a lazybones.

For Lord knows what he does that I dont know and Im to be slooching around down in the kitchen to get his lordship his breakfast while hes rolled up like a mummy will I indeed did you ever see me running Id just like to see myself at it show them attention and they treat you like dirt I dont care what anybody says itd be much better for the world to be

governed by the women in it you wouldn't see women going and killing
one another and slaughtering when do you ever see women rolling
around drunk like they do or gambling every penny they have and losing
it on horses yes because a woman whatever she does she knows where
to stop

Someone had marked up Joyce's famous riff. Above
slooching, he wrote *slouching?* And he underlined *governed*
by the women in it. Maybe not he. Edith? Helen? Such a
funny habit, underlining. The point is to mark
territory: Remember this place! Later, you come back
to the underlined passage and twist it in support of an
argument. Reading as a means to an end: an essay.
Underliners beget essay-writers. Essay-writers take an
author's words and put them to work, turning their
potential into kinetic energy.

Katherine Smith stares at the electric alarm clock,
waiting for it to ring. *Ring. Why don't you ring?* At 7:05 she
wonders what's gone wrong. Oh, Joe, her husband,
switched it off last night. It's Thanksgiving and he
doesn't need to wake up for work.

In a little while Katherine will get out of bed to
prepare an elaborate dinner. She'll make turkey with
orange-balsamic gravy. Chestnut stuffing. Cranberry
sauce. Mashed sweet potatoes. And something green:
asparagus. Two pies: pumpkin and chocolate pecan.

Katherine hears Joe snore, jostles him to make it
stop. The maneuver works. Later, Joe's brother,

Samuel, will come over with his family. Samuel's wife, Lisa, will offer to help in the kitchen, and Katherine will accept the offer, even though she prefers to cook alone and even though Lisa is incompetent and lazy as a spoiled cat. She, get this, doesn't even know how to chop onions. She cuts horizontal slices from the stem to the root, creating half-moons of varying sizes, some large, some small, which reduce unevenly. (Thanks, Edith, for the housewifey knowledge.)

Huddling under the covers, Katherine remembers that Lisa enjoys sampling dishes before they're ready. Everyone does this, but Lisa does this too often. Today, Katherine thinks, still in bed, Lisa will dip her pinkie into the orange-balsamic sauce. Then Katherine will reach for a butcher's knife. With a flick of the wrist she'll launch it at Lisa's pinkie and sever it at the knuckle. Samurai precision. Blood everywhere. Chop-chop-chop-chop. She'll remove the remaining four fingers on Lisa's left hand and drop them into a blender. Gross! *Vroom. Crunch.* Dinner is served.

If a Scholar's a Parasite

On the fourth day, against my better judgment, I called the only person in New Harbor who I thought might actually care that I was sick. She seemed genuinely distressed. It was Helen who came by, ran me a bath, changed my sheets, laid out a pair of clean pajamas, and prepared a can of vegetable soup — a paragon of selflessness. While I leaned against the pillows she'd arranged against the headboard, trying to eat lunch, she sat patiently by my side and urged me to rest, to nap as long as I could. When I woke up, she was going through my desk drawers. Through a haze I saw her open one after another. She uncapped a Montblanc fountain pen and held it up to the light from the window.

"What's it like outside?" I asked, my voice craggy from disuse.

"You're awake!" Helen exclaimed. She recapped the pen and put it back where she'd found it. "Cold and gray when it's not cold and wet. New Harbor gets more rain than Seattle, you know."

"Adds to my case that this is the worst place in America."

Arms folded across her chest, Helen looked out at the city that I had just disparaged — her home, not her way station en route to a degree. From her vantage point she could see the traffic on University Street and a slice of the green.

"It's a nicer place for you, at any rate, than for me," Helen said. "I get parks full of homeless people and pickpockets; you get lawns full of security guards. I live where I live, for now. You live — here."

"What do you mean, for now?"

"The landlord's an asshole" — *achoo!* "If I'm two days late paying rent" — *achoo!* — "he bangs on my door" — *achoo!* — "and threatens eviction."

My nurse reached for a tissue and released a fair amount of snot. She needed a second tissue to clean her upper lip and a third to get the stuff off her fingers. Had she sullied her sweater? Yes, a fourth tissue to remedy that.

"Did I get you sick?"

"Preexisting condition."

As I watched Helen maneuver, it occurred to me that she was almost old enough to be my mother. In parts of the country with high teen-pregnancy rates, exactly old enough. And on this occasion, she'd dressed the part: hair tied back in a rough bun, a shapeless black wool sweater, and boxy blue jeans that disguised her narrow, almost frail physique. My chest swelled with sympathy, a little-used feeling. She seemed so vulnerable. So weak. So unloved. I had discarded her, and she, not knowing my betrayal, had come to help me, a spoon-fed brat who lived in the grandest building in the city, while she had carpeting on her outdoor steps and unpaid bills in her shabby sitting room — which would be hers only so long, apparently, as her landlord tolerated her delinquency. My five hundred–dollar check hadn't helped that much. The feelings flowed up and out.

Helen put her hand on my shoulder.

"There, there," she said.

When I didn't stop, Helen pulled me up against her. In parts of the country with more liberal attitudes, she could have been my wife. I had never liked the sensation of breast-on-breast contact, and this was no exception, but I was rather enjoying the patting and maternal murmuring. It was the closest we'd been, physically, since she'd rubbed my rhomboids.

"There, there," she said again.

It was my turn to require Kleenex. I looked at the pile of wet and gooey tissues on the nightstand, her filth mixed with mine, and laughed, exchanging one convulsive, semi-controllable form of howling for another. Helen laughed too.

"Sickness is stressful," she said. "Or is something else going on?"

Professor Davidoff had asked me the same question, almost word for word, after calling my dissertation "a little thin." Haltingly and then breathlessly, I told Helen everything on my mind. That I'd had such a promising start, that my adviser thought I'd fallen behind, that my parents thought I was lazy or at least not maximizing my potential, that I was twenty-nine, that maybe what I really wanted was the life of a professor emerita—my wildest fantasy: having been a professor, not having to become one—nothing to do but snack, walk around, read, my present life, in short, without the need to finish a dissertation, like the story the homeless man told about the American banker and the Mexican fisherman, except unlike the homeless man, I could afford such a life, thanks to the original owner of the mahogany desk that sheltered the fountain pen Helen had admired, though that wasn't appropriate for someone my age, twenty-nine, almost thirty, and therefore I really did have to salvage my career, one way or another, so thank God for Frederick Langley's notebooks.

When I had run out of oxygen, Frederick Langley's niece said: "You make your situation seem dire and you make it seem complicated. But isn't there an obvious solution? Drop out of grad school. You don't really want to finish."

"Yes, I do," I protested. "I was born to do this. I'm in a rut, that's all. I want you to tell me to buck up, not quit."

"I can tell you whatever you want."

"After all, I'm so close. The notebooks —"

"Yes, yes, the notebooks," Helen parroted. There was a sharp edge to her voice that I'd never heard before. I could see that she was annoyed, but I didn't know what I had done to provoke her. She was still sitting right next to the bed, close enough that I could feel her breath when she sighed in exasperation. "Hasn't it occurred to you that they mean different things to us?"

"Of course. But you offered to pave the way for me so I could read them."

"I thought you might return the favor."

"By doing what?" I asked, bewildered.

"You could take my side in the lawsuit, write a letter to the judge as an expert witness."

"Gladly! I'll just finish my dissertation and then —"

Helen sighed again to cut me off again.

"Is it absolutely necessary that you help yourself before you help me? Don't you think that's a little selfish?"

"I have nothing to fall back on."

"Except your family's fortune."

"That's dishonorable."

"And studying English is honorable?"

"Don't you agree?"

"No. I think it's presumptuous. You presume to study writers, to use their creativity for your own ends."

She'd chosen her words carefully; they were IEDs tweaked for maximum damage. Now that it appeared we were having a full-on fight, I felt the need to improve my bargaining posture. I fluffed the pillows to give myself an extra inch or two in stature.

"That's the way of the world. There are authors and there are critics and there are scholars. There's literature and there's commentary. It's a symbiotic relationship. Joyce said he stuffed so many 'enigmas and puzzles' into *Ulysses* that it would 'keep the professors busy for centuries arguing over what it meant.'"

"Oh, fine, *Ulysses*," she said, drawing out the title mockingly. "First of all, I don't think he meant that kindly. Just the opposite, in fact. Besides, most books are not like *Ulysses*. Not every piece of writing requires analysis."

"Sounds like something an antiquarian would say. Someone who doesn't care about the contents of a book, only the dollar value."

"I'm not a moron, you know. I went to college. Fine, I didn't finish, but I went for a couple of years and I even took a few English classes. Then I gave that up. Not because it was hard. Because it was stupid. Professors spend their time pretending books written in plain language are as obscure as, let's see, as —"

"Hieroglyphics," I offered.

"Hieroglyphics. That's how they justify their salaries. Then they write their own books, books about books, that actually *are* as obscure as hieroglyphics and that no one reads. What a con. That's parasitism, not symbiosis."

"If a scholar's a parasite, if I'm a parasite, what's the word for you and your profession? I mean your real profession?" I paused to see if she'd play dumb or parry. She did neither. "I read that article about you. You lived off your uncle's money. You stole from your father. You defrauded your clients."

Helen receded, slumping into her chair as if she'd eaten something that didn't quite agree with her. Then she exonerated herself.

He Owed Her

In the summer of 1977, Helen's father, Thomas, announced to his family that his brother was coming for a visit. Freddy had been living in Europe for more than a decade doing God knows what. Not writing. He hadn't published a book since 1964. Not working at all, evidently, since Freddy had admitted quite freely that he'd run out of money as well as friends willing to lend him money and that he needed a place to stay. Hence the visit.

Thomas, a severe professional who wore a starched suit and collar every day to cow his patients, who'd never been in debt, who'd never borrowed money, was horrified by Freddy's behavior. In the days shortly after Freddy's arrival, the brothers kept Helen up at night with their fighting. What happened to Freddy's royalty payments? Thomas wanted to know. They'd dried up, Freddy responded. But they were never enough. Thomas called Freddy a spendthrift. Freddy, who relished the sonorous quality of repetition, called Thomas an uptight tightwad.

No one expected Freddy to stick around for long. A week or two. A month at most. Eventually he'd have to move on, wouldn't he? Find some kind of employment and an apartment of his own, right? On a few occasions Thomas nearly kicked Freddy out. On a few other occasions Freddy nearly walked out. Neither brother followed through. Perhaps three months in to Freddy's stay, Helen saw her mother, Edith, coming down from the attic with a carton full of nostalgic paraphernalia: photo albums, keepsakes from trips abroad, Helen's old dolls. She was making room for Freddy, who — she'd been the first to realize — wasn't going anywhere. Not that Edith was happy about her new housemate, but what could she do?

Helen was scared of her uncle. She'd overheard her father and mother discuss the possibility that he would be a bad influence on their impressionable young daughter. Eventually, though, curiosity drove her up the stairs to the attic, a chaotic place that she found restful by virtue of the contrast it presented to every other room in the house, because Helen's mother kept even the hallways and bathrooms in a state that she called "broker clean." Edith's interior-decorating style was best described as suburban anti-chic — throw pillows with inspirational sayings embroidered on the covers (*Success must be felt on the inside before it can be seen on the outside*, that sort of thing). Whereas Freddy had a habit of picking at the peeling paint on the attic walls and refused to make his bed or fold his clothes.

Freddy enjoyed having an audience. When his niece came to see him, he'd tell her stories about his childhood, his ex-girlfriends, his time in Europe. He'd also share what he called his "life philosophy," which seemed to amount to the idea that it was terribly burdensome, almost inhuman, to have a career, since careers made people think constantly about advancement instead of the *here and now*. Often he'd rant generally against middle-class values, taking particular aim at the bourgeois obsession with *self-improvement*. The term made him shudder. It made him imagine a person examining his self as if it were a kitchen that could use a new refrigerator. It was alienating. It was dehumanizing. He thought one should seek to know and explore one's self, not *upgrade* it. Even *betterment* was repugnant to Freddy. Why did people, at least modern people, value ascension over plateau?

Most of what Freddy said was either beyond the limits of Helen's childish understanding or Buddhist-influenced hippie pablum that sounded more poignant than it really was (she wasn't certain which). But she found her uncle wildly entertaining and would sit with him for hours.

"What do you two do up there?" Edith would ask.

"We just talk," Helen would say, even though Freddy always did most of the talking.

One afternoon when Helen went to pay Freddy a visit, she heard voices and hovered outside his door. Freddy was telling a story and a woman kept interrupting him with hysterical laughter. The woman, Helen understood, was her mother, yet she found it hard to accept this fact since she really wasn't the hysterical-laughter type. Helen went to her room. She flipped through a magazine. An hour later she walked back up the steps to the attic and found Freddy alone. He didn't mention his sister-in-law's social call.

Helen considered the incident an anomaly and put it out of her mind. But as Helen found out years later, it wasn't an anomaly at all. Edith, like Helen, would often make the climb to Freddy's room and listen to him expound. She'd sit on Freddy's bed while he'd wander and gesticulate like a maniac, waiting for him to join her. That set the mother's visits apart from the daughter's — the joining. Apparently, opposites attract. Apparently, Edith, the careful housewife with the broker-clean house who'd married an uptight tightwad, had developed a passion for the uptight tightwad's haphazard younger brother.

Was she overcome by an uncontrollable desire, or did she weigh disloyalty and its possible repercussions against what she wanted in the here and now and calmly choose the latter? Did she feel guilty? Did Freddy? Edith was betraying her husband, but Freddy, he was betraying his brother, his brother who'd welcomed him — albeit begrudgingly — into his home and was letting him live there rent-free. He was trespassing against the bonds of family and the ancient social dictum that a guest must respect his host and certainly not bang his wife.

It was no secret that the brothers were in conflict and had been since childhood, for which their father, Robert Langley, was chiefly to blame. Robert had set his sons against each other by making them compete for everything from his affection to holiday gifts. He would buy just one bike and present it to whichever son had a better report card; share his good bottle of whiskey with just one son, whoever had caught the most fish. Worse, Robert would give to one son what he'd taken from the other — Freddy's baseball cards to reward Thomas for cleaning out the garage. If everything had evened out in the end, with Freddy winning some contests, Thomas others, their father's eccentricity might have brought them closer together. But it was almost always Thomas, the steady, disciplined brother, who attained whatever carrot their father was holding out, while Freddy, the dreamy, free-spirited brother, got the stick. Was Edith payback? For the two brothers living under their father's roof as children, there had always been only one desired thing, not to share but to seize. For the two brothers living under Thomas's roof as adults, there was only one woman, and it was Freddy who seized her. In work, he'd never wanted to compete; in love, he apparently did not mind.

The affair began in the fall of 1980 and continued until Freddy's car accident. Helen was tucked away at boarding school. After Thomas left for work, Edith would ready herself for her husband's brother, her daughter's uncle. She'd let down her hair, apply a thick coat of red lipstick, and rub her limbs with cocoa butter. Then she'd knock timidly on Freddy's door. He'd tell her whatever nonsense was on his mind, and after a while she'd shut him up.

"How do you know all this?" I interrupted. "All these intimate details?"

Helen paused awhile to collect herself. She was laboring to switch gears, I supposed, from monologue to Q and A.

"I'll get to that. My mother said just enough, over the years, for me to reconstruct what happened."

Freddy never revealed the relationship to his niece, who learned of it only after his death, from her mother, and only because her mother had no choice. A neighbor had belatedly discovered the affair and threatened to go public. He didn't care that the information would devastate Thomas—his own brother! With his wife! Incest. Or at least a variant of that universal taboo. The neighbor didn't care that the media would pounce on such a salacious story about a well-known author and shame the whole family. And he didn't care that no good could come from the revelation other than the intangible good of truth for truth's sake. But he said he'd hold his tongue under one condition: if Edith paid him. Blackmail.

The main problem, among many other problems, was that Edith had no money of her own. She was a housewife with access only to a petty allowance that Thomas tracked hawkishly. He was certainly going to notice if Edith siphoned off cash earmarked for groceries and laundry detergent.

Edith told her daughter this sorry tale over the phone, weeping intermittently. Helen, at the time, was in Rome. She'd moved there instead of finishing college after inheriting part of her uncle's estate. Freddy hadn't exactly managed his money well, but after his death there'd been a burst of renewed interest in his work. His publisher reissued his three collections, and his stories were anthologized in student compendiums, yielding between fifteen thousand and twenty thousand dollars per year in royalties and licensing fees, of which Helen was entitled to half. Plus, a film studio bought the rights to — though never actually developed for the screen — "Longer" and "Lifetime Warranty," a onetime fifty-thousand-dollar windfall to which Helen was also entitled to half. Although it wasn't a fortune, it was enough for a thrifty escapade.

Certainly Edith knew the state of her daughter's finances when she spilled her guts. And when Edith asked, plaintively, "What should I do?" she had an answer in mind. Though stunned by her mother's incestuous — sort of — relationship, Helen felt she had no choice but to play the part of a dutiful daughter. She agreed to wire Edith everything she had and continue passing along Freddy's royalties for as long as necessary.

The cost of Helen's coerced generosity was her life abroad. Out of money, she came home to a grateful mother and a perplexed father. Thomas could not understand how his daughter had run into financial problems so quickly and was greatly disappointed by her behavior. She'd put off college for an adventure; that was bad enough. Then she'd spent so lavishly she'd had to cut that adventure short.

Thomas felt his daughter was incapable of managing her affairs and that he had to interfere — for her own good. In his home office, standing above his daughter while she squirmed in a straight-backed wooden chair, he insisted that she finish college. If Helen went to the University of Connecticut, Freddy's royalties should take care of tuition, but he'd gladly cover her living expenses if she promised to major in something practical, like premed or business or prelaw. When Helen didn't immediately accept, Thomas dipped into his straight-and-narrow arsenal of facts and figures: the grim economic prospects of Americans without college degrees, the advantages of setting out on a career sooner rather than later, the difficulty of getting back on the fast track after veering off course, the great self-worth Helen would assuredly feel, in time, with a BA on her cotton-stock résumé.

Helen, straining to find a comfortable position on that wooden chair, could not tell her father the truth: she'd willingly return to college but her father would have to pay for everything, because she did not have access to her uncle's royalties, because her uncle had been nailing her mother.

Instead, angry at the world, she pretended she was too bohemian, too much of a free spirit to do as her father wished. She said she did not want to major in something practical because she had no intention of doing something practical with her life. Whatever joy or basic pleasure there might be in working, Helen argued, would be extinguished by having to do so in the context of a career.

There was something confining and even morbid about that word, *career*, wasn't there? She knew from studying Latin in high school that it meant "course" or "road." She did not wish to live on a "course," and especially not a fast one—a fast track. That made life seem like a journey from point A, birth, to point B, death. It didn't have to be that way. One didn't have to aim toward death but could instead wander through the present at a leisurely pace, taking one's time. She continued in this vein for a while, concluding with the observation that she was not a kitchen in need of a new refrigerator.

Her father stayed silent through this condescending disquisition, which he considered nothing more than lefty bullshit and which he recognized had more than a touch of the late Freddy's outlook. In fact, Thomas saw in Helen the reincarnation of Freddy without the genius. She had Freddy's nose and Freddy's ears. She'd spoken like him. She'd fled across the Atlantic Ocean like him. After a point, Freddy had done precisely nothing with his life. Helen seemed eager to embrace nothingness at an even earlier stage. What could he do to break the pattern?

He figured that Freddy had collapsed—as a professional, as a human being—because he'd had it too easy. Without a rent-free roof over his head in Milford, he might not have thrown away his last years, rotting in an attic and corrupting a young girl. He would have had to do something, something fruitful. Now it was Helen who had it too easy. And so it was that, acting out of anger but telling himself that he was motivated only by love, Thomas gave Helen an ultimatum: Go back to school, or get out and fend for yourself. Helen chose the latter.

If Thomas had known that Helen didn't have Freddy's royalties to fall back on — if he'd known every penny was going to Edith — would he have acted so harshly? Certainly not, but Helen remained loyal to her mother.

On her last day at home, Helen sat with her duffel bag in her parents' sitting room, waiting for a cab that would take her to a train that would take her to New York — and a cash-strapped future. She was quite alone. Across from her father's armchair was a shelf full of Freddy's books, first editions and foreign-language editions and rare, illustrated editions. Helen looked and looked and felt more and more resentful of the man who had written those books, the man responsible for her plight. He owed her.

Helen made enough money from her initial batch of sales to buy more old books, and thus began her career as an antiquarian. The first year was rough. She may have forged her uncle's signature on a title page once or twice to pay the rent. But soon enough she developed a reputation as the sort of person who could quickly and reliably track down rarities.

Everything was going fine until the day Helen received a call from a stockbroker in Greenwich, Connecticut, who wanted to offer his daughter a first printing of *Washington Square* as an eighteenth-birthday gift. Helen explained that these were very, very difficult to find, but the stockbroker was very, very insistent. She tried her usual haunts but came up empty-handed, upsetting the stockbroker, who said he couldn't understand why she'd come so highly recommended. He was used to getting his way.

Panicked, anxious that her future was on the line, Helen

purchased a Book Club edition that looked just like the real thing, then doctored the copyright information and stained the pages with a teabag to make them seem older. Although the trick was unethical, Helen knew that her client and his daughter would admire the ersatz first printing, which they would assume was authentic. It would bring them pleasure. And it would bring Helen a tidy profit. So what? Her crime, she reasoned, ranked below palm reading in the hierarchy of fakery.

The stockbroker was duped, and pleased. Helen was pleased, and emboldened. Buying and selling old books was a low-margin business. Buying new books and pretending they were old — now, that was a high-margin business. She couldn't believe how easy it was to fool people. No one seemed to have any idea how to spot an imitation. But, predictably — how else could the story end? — she eventually sold a fake to someone who *could* spot an imitation,[3] and he wasn't amused, and he called the police.

---

3   *Life in the Cage*

At that time she lived in Prospect Heights, Brooklyn, on the second floor of a brownstone not far from the express train to Manhattan. Visitors would have assumed that she was an intellectual. It wasn't just the location of the apartment or its tin ceilings or its well-preserved wood cornices — all markers for the kind of person who in more earnest times was said to value the life of the mind. The dead giveaway was the great quantity of books lining the walls, divided carefully according to category — novels, poetry, plays, biography, history, journalism, criticism — then organized by publication date. But that dead giveaway led visitors astray. She'd acquired her collection at estate sales, library fire sales, and antiquarian conventions for purely financial reasons. She almost never read the words inside the covers. To her, books were merely objects whose value was determined by what other people were willing to pay for them.

The eighteenth-century antiquarian Sir Richard Colt Hoare once explained that he spoke "from facts, not theory," which was a sort of mantra for his professional descendants. Antiquarians never asked *What does this mean?* Instead they asked *What is this made out of?* and *How was it made?* and *Who owned it?* and *Who sold it?* The Italian historian Arnaldo Momigliano said that an antiquarian was "a type of man who [was] interested in historical facts without being interested in history." That was something less than a backhanded compliment, but it was accurate.

On weekday mornings she would fix herself coffee and toast in her slip of a kitchen. She would drink her coffee and eat her toast by the window overlooking a quiet side street. Then, abandoning her dishes in the sink, she'd approach the desk where she did her work.

Sometimes customers came to her for touch-up jobs — sturdier spines, for instance — to extend the life of their libraries. More often she reviewed requests for specific titles that came to her through intermediaries, usually bookstore owners, or directly from clients she'd helped in the past. If she happened to own the edition in question, the transaction was simple enough. If she didn't, she'd refer to her catalogs, such as the one distributed by the Antiquarian Booksellers' Association of America, which kept track of what was available, and where, and for what price. She'd assess what was feasible. Or she'd find a more imaginative solution.

When her friend at Argosy called to say that a customer wanted a first edition, first printing of Henry VanderMeer's *Life in the Cage,* she said she'd see what she could do. She understood that he wasn't talking about the serialized version, published in three parts in the *Pictorial Review* in 1919, but the hardbound edition later released by D. Appleton and Company in New York and London. She tracked down three available copies in the region, two of which were in excellent shape, both of which cost more than three thousand dollars. The ABAA catalog helpfully supplied a photograph of the copyright page. She also learned that look-alike editions released in 1955 were widely available for a mere two hundred and fifty dollars.

She wore the scarf her mother had given her years earlier, an ornamental thing not meant for warmth, made out of silk, yellow with white fleurs-de-lis, purchased on a trip to Paris. The trip had taken place in the time before. Rather, the time during but before anyone knew about it. It was the knowing that had changed everything, not the action. Adam and Eve ate the apple. They were punished only when God saw that they were ashamed.

She waited in the dingy station for the train that would take her to the Upper West Side of Manhattan. The bench was empty but seemed too dirty to tolerate. The trash can overflowed with paper cups. She looked up and saw rusty pipes and painted beams where, in other cities, she might have found a tiled roof. A triumph of function over form, some said. Once on the train, she stared at the promotional poster for *Basic Instinct*.

The man lived in an elevator building on 106th Street. She was surprised, when he opened the door, to see his side curls and untrimmed beard. Somehow she didn't associate VanderMeer with Orthodox Jews, though she'd never actually read VanderMeer, so possibly there was a clear connection that escaped her. He did not shake her hand — a religious thing, she figured — but otherwise he welcomed her warmly and had no objection to sitting alone with her in his living room.

"May I see it?" he asked.

She removed the book from her purse and set it on the low wooden table between them. It was covered in brown paper.

"I won't unwrap it yet," he said, steepling his fingers. "I'm too excited."

"One of your favorites?"

"I love VanderMeer. He's an author who deserves not only to be read, and to be reread, but to be re-reread. A wonderful stylist. The closer you pay attention, the more you'll appreciate his genius."

In her neighborhood, there was a kosher diner that attracted a mixed clientele, secular and not. Sometimes she saw Orthodox men in there reading the Bible, moving their lips as they went. She figured that was good practice for rereading and re-rereading VanderMeer. But she told herself that such behavior made more sense if the author was God and the text holy than if the author was an early-twentieth-century Bostonian, and the text — well, even granting the text was *genius*, it seemed a little much.

"Do you know the story?" he asked.

"It's been a long time," she mumbled.

"A pity. Do you mind if I —"

Thinking he meant to finally unwrap the book, she felt the usual flutter of anxiety that he'd notice something amiss. But no one had ever noticed anything amiss. Actually he was asking permission to tell her the story of the novel.

"*Life in the Cage* follows Julian, a young man from a rich Boston family who won't commit to a wedding date with his fiancée, Nancy. She's a lovely girl, well brought up, wealthy, but Julian finds her dull. The reader realizes that the best thing — for everyone — would be for Julian to break things off. But Julian keeps telling himself that he loves Nancy, that he just wants to

What happened next was part of the journalistic record; that *Town and Country* article was accurate enough. Thomas paid for his daughter's defense, but she was found guilty and sentenced to community service. Then Thomas used the conviction as legal grounds to take full control of his brother's estate, which he'd initially split with his daughter out of kindness (and for tax purposes). Helen had stolen her father's Frederick Langley collection and sold it off to launch her criminal career. Given her moral failings and obvious disregard for her uncle's work, Thomas's lawyers argued, Helen no longer deserved to profit from his talent. The judge agreed.

Not mentioned in the article was that Thomas's actions deprived not only Helen but also Edith of a rather important source of income, that Edith still refused to confess, and that the blackmailer,

---

savor his bachelorhood a bit longer, and that he'll eventually get around to tying the knot. You remember as much?"

"More or less," she said.

"There's another young man who does want to marry Nancy: Bill. He doesn't love Nancy either. But, unlike Julian, Bill needs Nancy's money. So he goes to work. He tells Julian that Nancy secretly wants to remain independent. She wants the freedom to run her own affairs and shudders at the notion of raising children. It's not absolutely clear if that's false or not. Possibly Bill is onto something. And the reader never hears from Nancy, so there's no definitive answer.

"Because Julian *wants* to believe Bill's story, he does, and he simply overlooks the well-known fact that Bill has been hunting for a rich wife. When Julian next sees Nancy, he allows himself to interpret her words and actions in such a way that they conform to Bill's narrative.

"The ending is quite famous. Julian jilts Nancy, telling himself he's serving her interests, not his own. He celebrates with Bill. The next morning, Bill asks Nancy to marry him, and she accepts. A blindsided Julian walks around Boston, not quite understanding what's happened. He wonders if there's some way for him to convince Nancy to embrace the life he, oddly, is still convinced she wants. A life of solitude."

recognizing the old ways were coming to an end, had demanded one last payment. Just one last payment, and he'd shut up forever. Thus Edith convinced her nephew Ian to advance her quite a lot of money in exchange for a slight adjustment to the will she cosigned with her husband. Ian, not Helen, would inherit the house in Milford. If Thomas was surprised that Edith was willing to punish Helen even from beyond the grave, he didn't say. More likely he accepted unquestioningly that his wife had come around to his view of their wayward child, and not having any nieces or nephews of his own, he had no objection to helping Ian.

Poor Helen: Not an inherited penny to call her own. All because of her uncle and one parent's original sin. First her mother died; then her father. Ian got the house. Charities got her father's money. Freddy's publisher got Freddy's copyright. Helen got nothing. When she learned that the Elston Library had acquired her uncle's notebooks, she felt wronged yet again and spurred to remedy her estatelessness by clawing them back. She'd lost everything else. In this one matter, she was determined to win. Even if she lost the lawsuit, which everyone told her she would, she would find a way.

The Notebook

It is very unsettling to watch an adult eat a Twinkie. Edith must be going through menopause because she plowed through an entire carton of Twinkies in a single week. I felt tempted to use an exclamation point just there. Fine, I may have spent too much time in Europe, but, but, but there is something wrong with the country that created the Twinkie. I have a theory that Twinkies pass through the human digestive system intact and that they look exactly the same coming out as going in. Another possibility is that they reconstitute in the large intestine. Still: same out as in.

Scott is born with a silver spoon in his mouth and he trades it in for gold. He takes his substantial inheritance and invests it in the stock market. His fortune grows and grows. Scott's daddy is very proud, very proud, 5 percent prouder with every 5 percent gain. What does it matter that dear Scott's successful because he's ruthlessly amoral? Ruthlessly immoral? Because he backs companies that produce missiles and machine guns? Because he encourages these companies to sell weapons to South American psychopaths? Daddy's so proud he gives Scott even more money than he initially promised. The origin of these funds? Money set aside for Scott's siblings, who aren't quite so driven.

He was so very unhappy when I stopped. He wasn't happy when I chose what I chose but he accepted it eventually because he saw the royalty checks, saw the reviews, and liked to tell his friends in Concord, *That's my boy.* I hated his approval as much as his disapproval. Having come around to writing, he could never come around to the end of it. He could not understand it. He could not accept it. No amount of time could make a difference. Now he's an old man. Now he's a sick man. One day I will have to speak at his funeral. Revenge is a dish best served in front of a cold body. Should I mention the time I asked for a kite for Christmas, a red kite for Christmas, and he bought one, and he showed it to me, and then he gave it to Thomas because Thomas cleaned out the gutters while I slept in?

Thomas caught me at the back door throwing rocks and asked me to pick up a gallon of milk from the supermarket. I said no. We fought. I said I would but I didn't have any money. We fought. He gave me five dollars and told me to bring back three dollars and thirty-eight cents. When I arrived there was a crowd blocking the entrance. A labor dispute. The protesters adhered rigorously to the classic demonstration aesthetic, from their handmade signs to their faded jeans to the sincerity with which they called out slogans. Just looking at them exhausted me. I bought milk as requested, paid like a model citizen, strolled peacefully outside, whistled, launched the open milk carton at the protesters, and ran. Got away clean. Gave Edith the three dollars and thirty-eight cents and told her to buy herself something special before sneaking upstairs.

"You look as fresh as a rose today, dear."
"I bet you say that to all the girls."
"Jane, you are my one and only."
"Are you trying to butter me up, Dick?"
"No need for butter, you are the crème de la crème."

Dear Diary, writes sixteen-year-old Amanda, *no one will ever read these words but I.* What purity! What grace in a girl so young! Amanda shares everything with diary dearest—her first kiss, her first lay, her first cigarette. The twist: She leaves the diary where she knows her younger sister, Patricia, will find it. Every phrase is a boast or an insult meant for a very particular audience. *Dear Diary, I wish Patricia wouldn't wear those headbands. They make her look fat.*

Dad said stop writing in that diary and do something. Journal. As a boy I called it a journal not a diary.

Diaries were for girls. Idle! Hands! Not idle at all, holding a pen, I said. Worse than empty, he said.

A man and a woman share their deepest, darkest secrets over the course of a long train ride. Such a relief to find a confidant, each thinks. Then why is it each goes home feeling empty, drained, not at all rejuvenated? *The Berlin Stories, La bête humaine, Strangers on a Train, A Sport and a Pastime, Franny and Zooey, The Natural* all begin on trains or at train stations. Maybe I'll teach a seminar: Narrative in Motion. Would anyone hire me to teach? I saw a copy of *The Berlin Stories* downstairs.

My first impression was that the stranger's eyes were of an unusually light blue. They met mine for several blank seconds, vacant, unmistakably scared. Startled and innocently naughty, they half reminded me of an incident I couldn't quite place; something which had happened a long time ago, to do with the upper fourth form classroom. They were the eyes of a schoolboy surprised in the act of breaking one of the rules. Not that I had caught him, apparently, at anything except his own thoughts: perhaps he imagined I could read them. At any rate, he seemed not to have heard or seen me cross the compartment from my corner to his own, for he started violently at the sound of my voice; so violently, indeed, that his nervous recoil hit me like a repercussion.

Angelica and Heather, co-workers, meet daily for tea in the break room. A friendship develops, and to Angelica it's a thing of beauty. Poor Angelica. The affection's all on her side, but she's too stupid to realize it. Finally Heather weaves her web: "He wronged me, Max did. He stole my [jewels or Maltese Falcon or Thunderbird; it doesn't matter]." Angelica hems and haws but comes around in the end: "I'll do it. I'll get [them/it] back." Oh, but [they/it] was not stolen at all! There's only one thief in the story, and it's Angelica.

Like a Mute Animal on an Operating Table

Mr. Richard Anders

c/o Finer and Bloch

90 West 7th Street, 10th Floor

New York, NY

Dear Richard,

I understand that you were Freddy Langley's book editor. I'd like to ask you a few questions about him.

[No. Go formal.]

Dear Mr. Anders,

I understand that you were Mr. Frederick Langley's book editor. I am a graduate student in English at Collegiate University who is studying Mr. Langley's work, and I am writing to ask for your help in answering a few questions. Your former employer's receptionist was unwilling to give me your current address and claimed that you do not use e-mail. But she promised she'd

forward my letter. I suspect she opens your mail. Still, I trust
that she'll send this along promptly.

[Warily, I opened the refrigerator. Nothing. I closed it. I opened it.
It was, on closer inspection, rich in condiments: brown mustard,
mayonnaise, ketchup, soy sauce — did soy sauce even require
refrigeration? It was also rich in foods similar to condiments:
anchovies, capers, precut sweet-and-sour pickles that I'd bought
by mistake. (I hadn't noticed the *sweet-and-* on the label.) The pickles dated back to the day, months ago, when I'd paid for Helen's
groceries. I closed the refrigerator again. I opened it again. Strawberry jam and peanut butter. No; the jar for the latter was empty. I
checked the crisper: celery.]

Something you said in *Freddy Remembered* stuck in my mind: that
Mr. Langley found the "Lifetime Warranty" mania "funny." At
first, I assumed you meant funny in the straightforward, *ha-ha*
sense of the word — that it amused him. All that ink spilled for a
story you described, aptly, as a trifle! But were you driving at
something a little different — that he found the response *strange,*
that it bothered him, even? Although I am a graduate student, I
understand perfectly well that it can be unpleasant for a writer to
find himself under the knife, like a mute animal on an operating
table, unable to protest.

[Too much? *Kill your darlings* applied only to fiction. From my window I contemplated University Street, gradually illuminated by
headlights and streetlights as the sun sank on the horizon. In big

cities, like New York or Los Angeles, nighttime invited reflection on one's insignificance. All those brightened windows. All those people living their lives, raising families, aging, getting depressed, getting sick, feeling joy, or just watching television, knowing nothing at all about you, safe inside an apartment building somewhere — it was sobering. Likewise, in rural areas, the stars made one feel small, intergalactically small, *Oh my God, I'm a speck in time and space* small. New Harbor, though, wasn't large enough to buzz with human energy or tiny enough to let in the universe (those headlights and streetlights were enough to obscure the Milky Way). Looking out made one — made me — look inward.

This was unpleasant. I was churning with frustration. Twice before, I'd tried to write a letter to Anders, never getting it right. There was too much I wanted to ask. I had granular questions about certain stories: Why won't the mayor run for a fourth term in "Omega"? Was Langley echoing the apocryphal Hemingway story "For sale: baby shoes, never worn" in the ad written by the old maid in "Baby Crazy"? I also caught myself pushing for slice-of-life anecdotes. Did he tell good jokes? Did he talk about his love life? Was he charming at parties? I told myself that such details would help me understand Langley's disposition as a writer, but I knew in truth I was just curious. I was growing attached to Langley in the way Evelyn grew attached to fictional characters — and that childishness would help my dissertation not at all. I had to stay focused on what was useful.]

I apologize for having spent so long on just one word. My academic training is to blame. But Mr. Langley's meaning seems important since it was around this time — after publishing "Lifetime Warranty" — that he cut short his career, and I'm eager, for professional reasons, to understand why. As best as I can tell there are three possible explanations for his silence: (1) He wanted to go out on a high note, the high note being "Lifetime Warranty"; (2) he had writer's block; (3) he developed a quasi-Buddhist antipathy to public notice.

[I applied jam to a celery stalk, longing for peanut butter. It was a noxious combination.]

I am also eager to understand — also for professional reasons — why Mr. Langley returned to writing so many years after "Lifetime Warranty." Of course I'm alluding to the notebooks he kept while in Milford. And that brings me to my second question.

[Arms up; chest out. Better to draw attention to it or ignore it? Anders wouldn't notice that I was trying to use him for semiotic grunt work — better to ignore. Actually, he probably would, since he was an editor.]

And that brings me to my second question, which, oh dear, also involves close reading, though of two words rather than just one. Twice as many the second time around, if we're counting!

Shortly before he died, Mr. Langley told Helen Langley, his niece, to "look after" his notebooks. What do you think he meant by that, *look after?* At any rate, he must have been worried about what would happen to the notebooks. Otherwise, he wouldn't have said anything at all. So why wasn't he more explicit? I'm aware that he died suddenly, in a car accident. Nevertheless, it seems to me he could have left his affairs in better order.

[Arms up; chest out. In my old age I would hobble with my back bent over like any number of punctuation marks. Comma was the usual comparison but the question mark or semicolon worked just as well. My head was the dot. Arms up; chest out. Finish it.]

Please respond at your earliest convenience.

Yours sincerely,
Anna Brisker

The Notebook

Dearly beloved, we are gathered here today. (Or is that for weddings? Is it possible that's for weddings and funerals both?) Dearly beloved, we are gathered here today to celebrate or grieve, depending on your point of view, the passing of Robert Langley, a strict man, hard-hearted, shaped if not scarred by the Depression—but not in the traditional sense. It wasn't poverty that made him. It wasn't knowledge of hunger, cold, shame. No, no, dearly beloved gathered here today, it was the opposite: well-being.

The day of the stock-market crash he was a young man, eighteen years old, newly enrolled in college. His family had already paid the tuition in full. So while others lost their jobs, he studied. Soon he met Elizabeth, the daughter of a Presbyterian minister who ran a school in Concord and who was looking for a successor. So while others waited in breadlines, he waited for his father-in-law to die. She died first. I should point out that she died first. But he weathered the loss like he weathered the Depression: high and dry. (I never saw him cry.)

Others might have attributed such smoothness in rough times to luck. Others might have felt guilty. Not Robert Langley. No, oh no. Robert Langley figured— no, oh no, knew that his strength of character was the source of his good fortune. If he had a good job and good money it was because he deserved it. If everyone else didn't, it was because they did not deserve it. If he gained while others lost, that was quite right.

Quite right. And therefore FDR was quite wrong. He hated the initialed man. He thought the New Deal, and in particular unemployment insurance, was a rebellion against the natural order and that any and all economic interventions in the name of assisting the downtrodden could only muddy the waters. Help the unfit? Take from the successful? What arrogance. In the 1936 presidential election, he voted for Alf Landon.

Robert Langley's outlook did not align with eye-of-the-needle Christianity, which was a bit of a problem, beloveds, seeing as he was headmaster at a Presbyterian school. But he rationalized his beliefs by putting special emphasis on John, chapter 3, verse 2, which read: "Beloved, I wish above all things that thou mayest prosper and be in health, even as thy soul prospereth." There was nothing particularly Christian about penury. As John revealed, God was only too happy to reward His faithful followers with prosperity. All that said, one couldn't simply expect

God to peer into one's soul and, assuming He liked what He saw, rain down money. That was absurd. No, one had to work, and work hard, to prove one's worth. Malachi, chapter 3, verse 10: "Bring to the storehouse a full tenth of what you earn so there will be food in My house. Test Me in this," says the Lord. "I will open the windows of heaven for you and pour out all the blessings you need." The blessings you need—but earn and bring to the storehouse.

Every year on the first day of school and on the last, the same message. The parable of the talents. John, chapter 3, verse 2. Malachi, chapter 3, verse 10. Idle! Hands! Didn't the other teachers notice? Forget the way he strained to make the words say what he wanted them to say, twisting and straining, didn't they notice how repetitive he was?

In parenting, Robert Langley expressed his tortured if practical theology by drawing a straight line from work to reward and from idleness to punishment. He had a system. Thomas and Freddy had various chores around the house and for these they were paid cold hard cash. Or at least cold hard coins. They each had a plot in the family vegetable garden and were paid to pull weeds. Ten for a penny. Well, well do I remember that feeling, the moment when the soil released the roots. Like popping a pimple or ejaculating. But excuse me, I digress. If they didn't pull enough weeds or wash enough dishes, they'd have to pay their father instead of vice versa.

But it was never "they" who failed; it was always
Freddy, not Thomas. Picture this recurring scene:
Robert finds Freddy daydreaming in the garden while
his older brother sweats. Robert demands Freddy's
pocket change, which he then gives, ceremoniously, to
Thomas. They fuck you up, your dad and bro. Larkin
said they may not mean to, but they do.

Dearly beloved, there was just one thing Freddy did
better than Thomas, and everyone knew it, though
Robert didn't care, didn't think it mattered, didn't
think it was serious, didn't really think it was work at
all. He was onto something. What was sitting around
for hours and hours and hours waiting for inspiration
if not nothing? It wasn't something. It wasn't work.
Especially not if it came so easily. A refuge from profit
and loss. He ruined that too. When the critics
discovered me — like Columbus discovering America,
I was already there! — he decided it was worthy after
all. So it wasn't. He ruined that too.

Ura Joke

Students darted across Elston Plaza like swallows. Or mice? Something small. Like Red Square or Tiananmen Square or other Communist expanses, Elston Plaza was not designed at human scale. It was the opposite of intimate. An L-shaped colonnaded building with a rotunda at the joint took up the base and the northern leg. In its shadow, pedestrians looked weak and pesky. They begrimed the stark cleanliness of the white granite pavement. At the top of the plaza was the library, a cube rising out of a sunken courtyard on four massive stone piers that, from certain angles, appeared to float. No windows defaced the cube, but all four sides were partially transparent. Thin, white marble panels framed in granite let in filtered, golden light.

Inside the cube was another cube, this one made of glass and filled with books: the Elston's closed stacks. The library seemed premised on the idea that books required protection from humans. In fact, it was well known that engineers had installed an unusual fire-extinguishing mechanism. At the first sign of smoke, it sucked air out of the building and replaced it with halon gas, which would stifle the flames and, incidentally, suffocate anyone left behind.

Security was tighter than at the other campus libraries, as was natural, given the value of the collection and the fact that the volumes never circulated. As I waited in line to pass through a turnstile under video surveillance, a swallow or a mouse gave me one of those looks that might have meant *You were my TA. You gave me an A minus. How dare you?* Or *Will I ever be so old?* I didn't recognize her but I did imagine that I could recognize in her the boundless arrogance of an intelligence not yet stopped in its tracks for repairs. Although I felt nostalgic for that phase of life, I also felt, to stick with the same metaphor, that I was almost back on schedule.

After showing the guard at reception my student ID, I went downstairs to the main reading room. A second guard at a second reception area had me sign in, then waved me through without further bureaucratic rigmarole. He was impatient to finish reading the sports magazine on his desk. I was feeling cheerful and almost stopped to banter, but I wasn't sure whether I should drop the name of a New England or New York team. New Harbor sat directly on the fandom border, its citizenry divided against itself.

A dozen or so people occupied the reading room. Thanks to a glass fourth wall, the room had a human-aquarium vibe. It felt private, though; it was several meters below grade and faced the sunken courtyard. Only if we pressed close against the glass could we catch bits of the city beyond, and I didn't think anyone at street level could see inside. The courtyard housed a modernist sculpture garden. I could not remember the name of the artist — Japanese? — who'd built the centerpiece, a black cube balanced on one point, but I knew that it was meant to signify chance. Cubes within cubes looking out on cubes. Most of the visitors were bent over their texts in heady dedication. A few stared dreamily at the geometric objects outside. I thought of a more traditional but sassier sculpture in Golden, an impish stone figure with a book on his lap grasping a frothy mug of beer. The open page read URA JOKE. It channeled the way many if not most artists felt about academics.

I spotted Dr. Kristen Lambert—that is, a woman who looked just like Dr. Kristen Lambert's head shot on the Elston website. She had mousy brown hair and generous breasts tucked beneath a ratty cardigan. Her short little legs emerged from her wool skirt like fat loaves of bread from a brown paper bag. A librarian in a librarian costume; a librarian out of a comic book.

"You must be Anna," said Dr. Lambert.

We shook hands.

Invited to sit down, I took my place across from a flat metal container roughly the height of a shirt box. Dr. Lambert pried off the top with some difficulty and exhumed two black-and-white-marble notebooks. They were ordinary. I often used the same brand for research.

While the notebooks sat there, tantalizingly, Dr. Lambert delivered a speech in her best indoor voice. She wished the notebooks were generally available. She wished the Elston could sell the rights to a commercial publisher so the whole world would have access to Langley's last prose. It wasn't rare, however, for a grubby relative to come out of the woodwork and spoil things for everyone. Eventually, the university would triumph. On that point she was confident. Eventually, the grubby relative would lose. Until then, the university played by her rules.

I was instructed not to fold the pages, not to wet my index finger to turn pages, to keep physical contact with the notebooks to a minimum, since the oil on fingers was harmful, over the long term,

to paper. Dr. Lambert thought that was about all. When I was finished, I was to return the notebooks to the metal container and
deliver it to the security guard. I felt special. I was having fun.
How many people had read the notebooks resting in front of me?
Potentially they were a big deal, a real opportunity, I thought,
rounding things off with a disgusting carnivorous metaphor usually applied to virgin prostitutes: fresh meat.

"Utilize your time wisely," said Dr. Lambert in closing.

Utilize. That had to be the worst word in English, or at least the
least — ironically — useful, as it meant the exact same thing as *use*
but took longer to say and was therefore a definitively unwise utili-
zation of time. It was right up there with *explicate* for "explain."
Francis Goodman, I remembered, had used the word too, in his
efficiency lecture. Why would a man who prized split seconds favor
a three-syllable word when a one-syllable word would do just as
well?

After Dr. Lambert rode her loaves away, I stretched preemp-
tively in my usual manner, like an athlete preparing for a tough
game ahead, and reached for the notebooks. Langley had dated the
inside covers: *December 1978–October 1980,* and *November 1980–.*
The order, then, was obvious. I arranged a few pencils — no pens
allowed at the Elston — to the right of my yellow legal pad. *Tolle
lege,* I thought, full of pompous self-importance.

The Yellow Legal Pad

Notebook #1

Lewis is turned off. He decides not to share his
accomplishment. And suddenly he feels
wonderful. Elated. He doesn't understand but
what's happened is simple enough. What he
doesn't share belongs to him alone.

Luce understands that the desire to do nothing is
shocking to Americans.

That meddlesome man in Paris asked me why
once. Why was my career shaped like a cliff? Or
why not, more like. Why not just keep going? . . .
What a strange question, as if the most natural
thing once you've started is to never stop.

The lecture Dad most liked to give was on the
parable of the talents, which he preferred to the
parable of the prodigal son . . . It made no sense to
him that a father would reward a screwup
offspring . . . Our neighbors assumed he thought
up that "business-parenting" system of paying us

pennies for every completed chore . . . Nothing was ever done for its own sake.

I was like that. Easy-peasy lemon squeezy. Not a blot, not a messy pink eraser trace. All the struggle happened before the words ever hit the page.

Richard did not love "Lifetime Warranty" but I know I'll never write anything so good again, it was my peak, my high point, my crowning achievement.

Americans would not empathize with the third servant. No, not at all. Reap what you sow is the ethos of this great land stretching from sea to shining sea. Milton made the obvious leap from talent as coin to talent as natural ability.

Some lifetimes are meant for doing nothing. Nothing: the antidote to boredom. Nothing: the only pure pleasure.

The Protestant work-ethic aesthetic. It was all so long ago, so many decades. I'm old now, ought to just get over it. But childhood stays with you. Living with Thomas makes it fresh again.

Such a funny habit, underlining. The point is to mark territory: Remember this place! Later, you come back to the underlined passage and twist it in support of an argument. Reading as a means to an end: an essay.

Scott is born with a silver spoon in his mouth and he trades it in for gold. He takes his substantial inheritance and invests it in the stock market... Daddy's so proud he gives Scott even more money than he initially promised. The origin of these funds? Money set aside for Scott's siblings, who aren't quite so driven.

I hated his approval as much as his disapproval.

Dear Diary, writes sixteen-year-old Amanda, *no one will ever read these words but I.* What purity! What grace in a girl so young!

Dad said stop writing in that diary and do something.

A man and a woman share their deepest, darkest secrets over the course of a long train ride. Such a relief to find a confidant, each thinks. Then why is it each goes home feeling empty, drained, not at all rejuvenated?

In parenting, Robert Langley expressed his tortured if practical theology by drawing a straight line from work to reward and from idleness to punishment.

There was just one thing Freddy did better than Thomas, and everyone knew it, though Robert didn't care, didn't think it mattered, didn't think it was serious, didn't really think it was work at all. He was onto something. What was sitting around for hours and hours and hours waiting for inspiration if not nothing? It wasn't something. It wasn't work. Especially not if it came so easily. A refuge from profit and loss. He ruined that too. When the critics discovered me—like Columbus discovering America, I was already there!—he decided it was worthy after all. So it wasn't. He ruined that too.

Notebook #2

His True Intentions

"It was too absorbing to underline or take notes," I said. "All those nascent ideas and themes from the first notebook coalesced in the second notebook into a magnificent whole, like streams merging into a river," I added, getting carried away. "He wrote a pretty damn good novel."

A block or so from the Roosevelt, a former hotel, was an actual hotel, still in use. The dining room at the very top had a better view of the green than my apartment did. From our table we could also see First Campus, the quad where freshmen lived. Too late for early birds, too early for hotel guests with nightlife in mind, we were one of only three couples in the restaurant, a well-lit undivided room with large windows on all sides. The husband and wife looked over documents. The gay men held hands across the white tablecloth, then parted digits when they became aware of the bored bow-tied waiters. The bored bow-tied waiters arranged and rearranged the red paper napkins on the bar.

As for Helen: She picked at a loose thread on the orange trench coat she hadn't bothered to remove. It was one of her no-makeup days, which I preferred, even if in profile she looked insubstantial. Her lips were thin, her eyelashes stunted.

"When I read it, back when this all started, it seemed like a work in progress," she said. "It seemed rough."

"But he was well on his way and it's obvious what he had in mind: a rewriting of the parable of the talents. It's clear from the beginning, when the man at the baseball game says he plans to disinherit his lazy expat of a youngest son so that his older boys can benefit."

I felt embarrassed to remember how recently I'd caricatured Langley as an author for idiots who didn't like reading. Just because he wrote for everyone didn't mean he wasn't a genius. He deserved better than Helen's dismissive tone.

Once more Helen picked at the loose thread. She seemed impatient and annoyed. The notebooks meant different things to us, as she'd reminded me not long ago. They were heirlooms to her, material to me. My excitement could do nothing for her. What did it matter to her that I was feeling a sort of eagerness most normal people associated with the early stages of romantic love?

"You know," I said, determined to bring her over to my side, "it can't hurt your case to have me studying him. You said yourself you could use my expert testimony. If a respected Langley scholar, not just a gestating PhD, states in a court of law that in her opinion, the author would have wanted his niece . . . you see where I'm going. Let me tell you what I think about your uncle's notebooks and maybe something will stand out. Something useful to you."

Helen dropped the thread. She'd decided to engage, to indulge me, perhaps. I felt she would pay closer attention to my theories than Professor Davidoff had, though that was a low standard.

"I have two questions, if you don't mind," I said. "When did your uncle's affair with your mother start? And when did your grandfather die?"

"Around the same time — the fall of 1980. October was the funeral, and I don't know the exact date for the relationship but I think soon after."

"That's also when he started the second notebook, the one containing the novel."

It was all coming together.

Freddy, as we both understood, had a difficult relationship with his father and brother. This was attributable to the father, who'd pitted his sons against each other with a pay-per-chore system. This system was a daily realization of Robert's favorite parable in which Robert played the landlord, who stood in for God, taking from the wicked and slothful servant (Freddy) and giving to the good and productive one (Thomas). Robert's playacting extended beyond chores. He also forced competition in schoolwork and sports, again giving to the productive son what he took from the slothful one.

Helen knew all that. She also likely knew that if losing was painful to Freddy, so too was the stress of experiencing just about everything in his life as part of a grand rivalry with his brother. What I had to add to Helen's understanding was that Freddy had discovered an out: writing. This was pleasurable not just because he was better at it than Thomas but because his father considered it wholly frivolous and didn't integrate it into his system.

When Freddy described his artistic process, he cast himself as a natural who effortlessly conveyed words from thin air to the page. He said he wrote so fluidly he didn't erase a single word. And his college editor echoed these familiar phrases — tropes, really — in *Freddy Remembered,* claiming that his manuscripts arrived fully formed, as if delivered by stork. There was reason to believe this wasn't the whole story, however. In almost the same breath that Freddy bragged he didn't need an eraser, he admitted there was a struggle, just that it came before he put pencil to paper. Likewise, even as he pretended that writing came easily to him, he acknowledged that he sat around for hours at a time waiting for inspiration. Waiting, undoubtedly, was a form of work, an indication of discipline. And work, discipline, was the source of his stories — not a stork.

For thousands of years — I allowed myself to say — scholars and artists had sought to explain how writers produced writing, and they all pinpointed forces beyond the writers' control instead of looking to the obvious factors: work and discipline. But perhaps the better question, anyway, was why a person became a writer at all. What motivated him to create art instead of doing something more practical, like plumbing, or more lucrative, like investment banking? Motive. Motive was more germane than inspiration. And, returning to my subject, the motive was clear in Freddy's case. He wanted to escape that system of profit and loss that he found so burdensome.

(Incidentally, we also had a motive for why Freddy denied the undeniable truth that creative work was indeed work; it wouldn't have felt rebellious anymore.)

We knew why Freddy turned to writing. Why did he then turn away from it? The timing mattered. He retired after publishing his most critically acclaimed story, "Lifetime Warranty." Someone fixated on the question of inspiration would argue that success had spooked Freddy and caused him to lose his touch. But something more concrete had happened. He'd lost his motive.

Freddy told Richard Anders that he found the "Lifetime Warranty" mania "funny," meaning discomfiting. By pouncing on the story and elevating Freddy from a popular writer to a bona fide author, critics transformed writing from an amusing pastime into a job, one that met with Robert's unwanted approval, and one that Freddy then felt compelled to abandon.

For this sequence of events, we had plenty of evidence. Freddy's onetime girlfriend Rebecca Johnson recalled seeing Freddy in a dark mood when he was finishing *Omega* and went to see his father. Robert recognized that his son was doing well and he was therefore coming around to Freddy's fiction, which — to Rebecca's surprise — Freddy found irritating. In the first notebook, Freddy affirmed that his father had ruined writing for him when he — Robert — saw the positive reviews and decided that his son wasn't throwing away his life after all.

In brief, Freddy quit writing when it was no longer an escape but a career, something he did to make money, to please reviewers and his father. Whether or not he was trying to achieve these objectives didn't matter. That was the result.

So we also knew why Freddy stopped writing. Final question: Why did he return to it? Here again, the timing mattered. He began the first notebook soon after he moved into his brother's attic in Milford, perhaps, as Helen had once suggested, because he was bored. He began his more formal project, an actual novel, in November of 1980 — the month after his father died *and* shortly before he began his affair with Helen's mother.

These events were connected.

Freddy no longer needed to worry about writing for his father's approval because his father was dead. There was no unintentional, unwanted goal and therefore no impediment anymore. At the same time, Freddy developed a new motive: The desire to explain or justify his inaction. This Freddy did through the central character of the novel he'd drafted in the second notebook, a man in not only his image but also that of the wicked servant.

At the peak of his career as an architect, Jonah — the central character — drops everything and moves to Brazil, where he lazes in the sun, drinks, and, in the privacy of his rented bungalow, continues to design buildings. He refuses to convert his designs into real-world projects, however, because only if he works unteleologically and in secret can he feel joy. Architecture, in theory the union of practical science and art, is, in his hands, pure art. He's extracted the engineering. He draws and erases, draws and burns or tears up his work. The destruction fills him with an almost orgasmic sensation. Pleasuring herself in bed, Molly Bloom says, "Yes I said yes I will Yes"; Jonah, possibly doing the same, says, "No I said no I will Not." And the better the design, the more exquisite the feeling when he consigns it to oblivion.

Freddy set out to reclaim this sort of behavior; it wasn't wicked at all but a way to find happiness by separating art from reward. The only significant difference between Freddy and Jonah was that Freddy had actually stopped producing art for a while, whereas Jonah had continued but kept his work secret, in part by destroying what he made.

My guess was that as Freddy wrote his novel, which amounted to a zealous defense of talent-burying, he found himself dwelling on the past. And as he dwelled, he dredged up his old, never-resolved antipathy toward his brother and felt moved to finally win a competition: for Edith's affection.

Helen gave me a crooked grin.

"Well?" I said.

"Well, it's really thorough, really tidy. I'm impressed."

"Thank you."

"You're missing something, though."

"What's that?"

"The obvious conclusion!" She'd raised her voice enough to attract attention from our neighbors. The waiters in their ridiculous getups gawped in our direction. So did the straight couple. So did the gay couple. Did they think we were fighting? That we were breaking up? We were too far apart in age for mere friendship.

"I don't know what you mean."

"His true intentions. It's strange you didn't get there. You said yourself that Freddy's protagonist, Jonah, keeps his work private and destroys it."

"That's where they're different, yes."

"Why would you assume that?"

"Still lost."

"When Freddy told me to look after his notebooks, that's what he meant. That I should keep them private. He must have. You said yourself he didn't like praise from critics because it turned him into an author instead of just a writer. When my grandfather died, Freddy didn't have to worry about him anymore, but he still had to worry about critics, about all readers, actually. Writing for an audience, that's like investing talent. He couldn't have written that novel for an audience. It would have contradicted everything he believed."

I had to admit that Helen's argument made a certain kind of sense. Maybe. It wasn't just the "funny" comment that revealed Freddy's aversion to critics. He found Marxist interpretations and so forth absurd. In the first notebook he derided essay-writers for putting an author's words to work for their own devices, their own gain. If he refused to write with a goal or reward in mind, removing his father from the picture wasn't enough, was it? No, it wasn't. That was logical. Up in the Milford attic, Langley had become a sort of prophet of passivity and nothingness. To such a man, to such a prophet, it was sacrilege to turn potential into kinetic energy, as he'd put it. Maybe.

I thought about the era in which Langley had entered the literary scene. It was a time of intense change and intense activity in academia. Although the practice of analyzing literature was ancient— Aristotle's *Poetics*—university professors through the mid-nineteenth century limited themselves to religious texts and poetry written in Greek or Latin. Before then, one couldn't get a job on a college campus blathering about modern-language writers. (For example, Harvard didn't create its English literature department or name its first professor of English literature until the 1870s.) For a while, most members of this new vocation contented themselves with aesthetic judgments, straightforward interpretations of the authors' intentions and biographical work. Who was Chaucer? Was he better than Spenser? What did he want the reader to learn from the Wife of Bath?

In the mid-twentieth century—when Langley lived— academics got bored of that model. They decided that authors weren't as important as previously believed and that their intentions were beside the point. What mattered was the text, which existed independently. You could keep yourself busy for weeks reading about why an author's interpretation of his own work did not matter, but the two most important essays in this genre were "The Intentional Fallacy" by William Wimsatt Jr. and Monroe Beardsley, published when Freddy was a boy, and "The Death of the Author" by Roland Barthes, published shortly after Freddy ended his career. Junking the author—declaring that his take was no more valid than any other—freed up the criticism industry like junking the gold standard freed up monetary policy. No longer anchored to the writer's point of view, academics experimented with exotic approaches to the study of literature: new criticism, structuralism, poststructuralism, deconstruction, reader-response criticism, new historicism.

Each dogma had its adherents. Universities in this period were home to furious debates among earnest representatives from different schools of thought, each absolutely convinced of the rightness of his or her ideas and the stupidity, even dangerousness, of all others, like Christian sectarians in Elizabethan England. Still, just as all Christians accepted that Jesus was holy, pretty much all academics accepted that authors were not.

What did writers make of this trend? That is, the people producing the literature that academics were treating like cannon fodder? One dissident was Nabokov, who despite making a living as a professor for many years, ridiculed scholarly overreach in his novels. In *Pale Fire*, Dr. Charles Kinbote appoints himself editor of a deceased neighbor's 999-line poem. Instead of supplying actual commentary on the text or his neighbor's biography, Kinbote relates his own (very colorful, probably fictitious) history. Nabokov was suggesting that academics longed to replace writers, to assume their central role in literature. The author had to die so the critic could live. Granted, *Pale Fire* came out before Barthes's essay, but that turn of phrase was too good to pass up.

Nabokov told his son, Dmitri, to destroy his last, unfinished novel. When Langley told his niece to look after his notebooks, was he asking her to burn, bury, or otherwise destroy them?

"What you're saying is, he wouldn't have wanted me to read his notebooks?"

"Not you. Not anyone."

"If that's true — a big *if*, a huge *if*, Helen — the Elston shouldn't have them."

"I absolutely agree. Good thing I sued."

"And what if you lose?"

"I probably will," she said, echoing what Dr. Lambert and Professors Pippen and Davidoff had predicted.

And then Helen shared her plan B.

My first thought was a reference: *Strangers on a Train*, Hitchcock's exploration of the theory that perfect strangers can exchange perfect crimes. (If A murders B's wife, and B murders A's father, then neither will face suspicion because neither has an apparent motive.) Of course, the comparison was wildly inapt. Helen would do nothing for me in return. And although no one at the university, so far as I knew, was aware of my connection to Helen, I was already publicly tied to the notebooks. That was enough to land me on a suspects list. But what was most outrageous, seeing as rich white girls rarely went to prison, was the blitheness with which she expected me to put her needs — in fairness, her uncle's needs, as she understood them — above my own. If I did as she asked, I'd lose — actively cause to disappear — the material for the case study essential to my dissertation.

It was her very blitheness, though, that set me more or less at ease. Dangerous people were more careful, more manipulative. They disguised their desires and their intentions. Helen's directness was proof of friendship. Here was what she wanted for herself and for her uncle. Whether I complied was entirely up to me.

007: Golden Sorrow

In previous generations, a Collegiate doctoral candidate in English would have been well situated to join the intelligence services, or at least dabble in freelance espionage as a research analyst. Perhaps not a woman, but a man in my position in the 1950s would have been known and trusted by the boarding-school elites who became the clandestine elites, and he could have set aside his books to serve his country. Or he could have used service as an excuse if books weren't working out for him, career-wise. It was not considered odd to exchange New Harbor, Connecticut, for Washington, DC, or, more on the nose, Langley, Virginia — to swap decoding literature for decoding ciphers.

James Bond wasn't making that alternative of yore seem enticing, though. He seemed bored with the whole enterprise. There was only one movie theater in New Harbor, only one movie I hadn't yet seen — *007: Golden Sorrow* — and I wasn't getting what I'd expected. Apparently the studio had swallowed the preposterous notion that anxiety was more intriguing than action and had let the screenwriters heave the protagonist into the throes of a serious malaise.

Dressed in a soiled linen shirt, Bond tells the bartender that he's sick of breaking his body for Her Majesty. He's had enough of trade-craft, of legalized murder, of long days and long nights. It occurs to him that he's a prostitute twice over, one who kills and loves for money. And, yes, for honor. His honor and the honor of the realm. But he's retired now. He finds Bali sleepily peaceful and doesn't want to so much as set foot in Merrie Olde England ever again. He has shot his last villain, tailed his last car, stolen his last state secret, disabled his last ticking time bomb, sacrificed his last contact.

The bartender eyes the petulant British man and fixes him another martini just the way he likes it. Is this guy for real? If he's for real, isn't this confession a security risk? Probably he is not a spy, the bartender whispers to a sultry waitress. Nor was he ever a spy. Probably he is just another drunk *buleh* avoiding the dreary responsibilities he's accrued over a lifetime back home. White peo-ple accrue dreary responsibilities better than any other race in the world.

A man walks into a dark bar in the middle of the afternoon. It takes a minute for his eyes to adjust. There's something wrong. Something eerie, something uncanny, about this place. Is it the place, come to think of it, or the clientele?

Cue the throwback opening credits. Cue the young agent, a sexy female, sent to bring Bond back into the fold at all costs. England — no — the world's future hangs in the balance. The mis-sion is the mission. It doesn't matter. Terrorists have kidnapped someone who has information about something but the hostage isn't what he seems and neither is the chief terrorist, who has a his-tory with the British government and, indirectly, Bond, who has an obligation to help.

"An obligation?" asks Bond. "My contract expired."

The young agent knows just what to say: "Yes, an obligation. Not a legal obligation but a moral obligation to spend your life, your whole life, doing what you do best: retrieving information and neutralizing targets."

"You mean stealing and murdering?"

"If you must call it that, call it that."

"And what about what I want? What I desire? Does that matter at all? What if I want to drink myself to death here in Bali?"

I poured the last of my Raisinets into my tub of popcorn, striving to maintain a ratio of three popped corns to one chocolate-covered raisin. Butter, salt, and sugar. Gnarled, dimpled, and industrial smooth. Only a dentist could disapprove. Weeks later he'd spot a kernel casing, hold it up with a pick, and, like a detective enlightened by a bloody footprint, imaginatively reconstruct the crime.

"Anna, have you been to the movies recently?"

"What do you think?"

"Have you been flossing?"

"What do you think?"

Funny to me the way Sherlock Holmes always gets his man in the end ... All the clues the detective thought he'd uncovered were figments of his imagination.

This snack-sorting process was significantly more diverting than watching Bond complain. I missed the thoughtless Bonds, the thoughtless Bonds I'd seen as a child in thoughtless films that had taught me how to recognize and break down a narrative formula long before I knew people did such things for a living. (M assigns Bond a mission; Q provides the tech; the villain appears; Bond tries to kill the villain; the love interest appears; Bond seduces her; the villain captures Bond; the villain reveals his intentions as he tortures Bond; Bond escapes; Bond reunites with the love interest.) I missed the plots that were subordinate to the action sequences, which were vehicles for vehicular chases, which were in turn vehicles for selling vehicles. I missed the movies written by someone who'd driven a convertible across the Col de la Bonette with the top down and thought, *Huh, it's not just beautiful, it works the engine. Perfect setting for a chase!* And had built a movie around that epiphany.

Raisinets and popcorn consumed, I walked out early and went straight home.

The Roosevelt's newest doorman, Manny, looked uncomfortable in his uniform—artichoke green from pillbox hat to double-breasted jacket to patent leather shoes—like a tomboy forced to wear a frilly dress to church. I didn't blame him. Such getups were embarrassing even in Manhattan where doormen were common. In New Harbor, where they were not at all, the subtext was excruciating. While on duty, he belonged to the building's residents and we could play with him, dress him up like a doll. He was "our man" and he had to look sharp, or ridiculous, to impress upon our visitors that we had the power to make him look sharp, or ridiculous. The fact that he was Latino while the building's residents were all either white or East Asian made the class dynamics even more trying.

"Anna, right? Anna Brisker?" asked Manny. "Package for you."

Inside were two slick oversized paperbacks: *Writing Your Dissertation in Fifteen Minutes a Day: A Guide to Starting, Revising, and Finishing Your Doctoral Thesis* and *Finish Your Dissertation, Don't Let It Finish You!* No note, but I suspected my parents. This tactic was even more annoying than their last.[4] When I called my mother to complain, she feigned ignorance.

"I have no idea who sent those to you. Still, they sound intriguing, don't you think? Maybe you should give one of them a try?"

The Protestant work-ethic aesthetic. It was all so long ago, so many decades. I'm old now, ought to just get over it. But childhood stays with you.

I tried to make my mother feel guilty by claiming I'd worked all day long on an article for publication, a lie that propelled me to my desk and my yellow legal pad. But I found it impossible to make progress, to move from reading to writing. Helen's ideas nagged at me, as did Freddy's.

Such a funny habit, underlining. The point is to mark territory: Remember this place! Later, you come back to the underlined passage and twist it in support of an argument. Reading as a means to an end: an essay.

---

4   See footnote 1.

Julia Maria Lustgarten

Together we read about robberies. Because our process was so familiar to me — not too different from a standard lit review — it was easy to set aside moral questions. We were merely educating ourselves. Action felt distant, abstract, in the domain of possibility rather than inevitability. I felt more like a military historian researching an invasion than a military commander actually planning one. For the time being, I was only playing along, and Helen knew that.

I said our process was familiar. Yet it was also more haphazard and amusing than what I was accustomed to. Helen suggested I buy a copy — using cash, to be safe — of a recently published book called *Art of the Art Heist,* which, despite its lofty title, was a glorified encyclopedia containing blurb-length synopses of notable thefts. In either my living room or Helen's study we'd scan the entries and, when something stood out, track down a more detailed description. Since we confined ourselves to robberies committed in the United States in the past quarter century, we were usually able to find what we needed in newspaper or magazine archives. Often we'd read the reports aloud over tea and cookies, marveling at the variety of criminal experience. We marveled, too, at the variety of

storytelling techniques. Some writers lingered on physical charac-
teristics, others on psychological motivations. Some tried to draw
the reader in with heist scenes told from the perspective of a suspi-
cious observer, others turned thieves into sympathetic antiheroes.

On a weekday morning in June of 2005, an Elston librarian saw an
X-Acto knife lying on the floor of the main reading room. She
brought it to her supervisor, who stored it in her desk drawer and
walked directly back to the reading room. L. Moore Cornwell was
there, as he often was, a handsome, gray-haired man nearing fifty
who always wore a casual academic costume: tweed jacket, a button-
down shirt with no tie, loafers with no socks. But Cornwell was not
an academic. He was an antiquarian art dealer who sold maps out of
his offices in Manhattan and Martha's Vineyard. On his website he
claimed to own one of the largest collections of American maps in
the country, which included many exceptionally expensive, exceptionally rare items, like a 1743 plan of Boston. It was unclear how he
had obtained these items. Several times a year he visited the Elston
as well as other libraries throughout New England.

The supervisor called the head of security at the Elston, who
called the police. When Cornwell left the library a few hours later, at
around three o'clock that afternoon, a detective gave pursuit, following his suspect to the Collegiate Center for British Art. The detective
introduced himself and asked Cornwell if he'd spent the day at the
Elston. Cornwell said he had. The detective showed Cornwell the
X-Acto knife and asked if it belonged to him. Cornwell — bless
him — said it did. Could the detective look in Cornwell's briefcase?
Yes, he could. Why were so many maps in his possession? Because,

Cornwell said, he wanted to compare them with maps in the Elston's collection.

Cornwell and the detective returned to the Elston, where the supervisor informed the latter that a book handled by the former — Captain John Smith's *Advertisements for the Unexperienced Planters of New-England, or Any Where*, published in 1631 — was missing a map. It wasn't inside Cornwell's briefcase. But the detective noticed a bit of paper sticking out of Cornwell's jacket pocket. That was it.

Cornwell said the map belonged to him. He said he'd bought it on a recent trip to London. Did he have a receipt? No. Any confirmation of the purchase? No. The detective arrested Cornwell on the spot.

Local police called in the FBI. Agents assigned to the case figured Cornwell had been stealing for a while. They were right. Cornwell later admitted that he'd started in 2002 and that Golden Memorial Library had been his first target. He'd requested a first edition of the early-nineteenth-century text *The Garden and the Tower: Early Visions of the New World*, which contained fantastical maps of the Americas. Sitting at a long table with habitually unobservant scholars further distracted by their reading, he moistened a piece of string in his mouth and placed it along the inner edge of a map that disclosed the location of the Fountain of Youth. In a few minutes the paper was soft enough to tear silently. He folded the map so it could fit in his jacket pocket, left the library, and soon after sold it for seventy-five thousand dollars.

Later he switched to an X-Acto knife because it was so much faster. He stole from Collegiate's libraries, the Boston Public Library, Harvard's Houghton Library, the Newberry Library in

Chicago, the New York Public Library, and the British Library in London. In all, he stole ninety-seven rare maps valued at more than three million dollars. For that he was sentenced to forty-two months in prison, later reduced to thirty-six months for good behavior.

Julius and Maria Lustgarten née Schmidt immigrated to the United States from Germany in the 1930s when they saw which way the wind was blowing for Marxists. They had a background in theater, spoke excellent English, and revered moving pictures as a populist art form. No surprise they made their way to Hollywood.

When America entered the war, they wrote schlocky screen-plays about handsome Midwesterners battling fascism with brawn and plain good character. Sometimes they slipped in Marxist themes. Whether or not the producers realized it, "from each according to his ability, to each according to his need" was the message of the movie about the ragtag team of hale-and-hearty farmers who took down a Nazi spy cell in Nebraska.

The Lustgartens' political beliefs weren't really a problem until 1945, when the Seventy-Ninth Congress passed Public Law 601, which gave the House Committee on Un-American Activities a mandate to investigate suspected attacks on "the form of govern-ment guaranteed by our Constitution." In 1947 the committee held hearings into alleged Communist propaganda in Hollywood. This led the studios to start blacklisting artists, including the Lustgar-tens. Many artists on the blacklist left the United States or wrote capitalist-friendly scripts under pseudonyms. The Lustgartens found the first option too painful — they'd already crossed the

Atlantic once — and the second too shameful. Deprived of their livelihoods and depressed, they might have considered suicide if it weren't for little Julia, who was just five years old.

By 1950, the Lustgartens were worse than penniless. They were in debt. Capitalism. One of Julia's formative memories was of the bank holding an estate sale at her parents' Hollywood Hills bungalow. She cried as she watched strangers cart away her parents' belongings: their furniture, their jewels, their antique silverware, and their entire library of precisely 307 books. When the bank agents left, they gave Julius an itemized list of everything they'd sold and to whom, along with the price paid for each. In exchange for a life, the family got a list.

Julius and Maria died within months of each other in 1971, when Julia was twenty-nine. Grieving and seething with bitterness, Julia carried the List with her everywhere she went; it served as a constant reminder of the tragedy that had befallen her family — and it aggravated her bitterness. Eventually she decided to avenge her parents by re-appropriating every last item on the List. Their library had been sold to a single buyer, California State University, Northridge, which she figured was a good place to start.

Julia's method was time-consuming, costly, and positively lunatic. First she used the Northridge card catalog to determine the edition numbers of her parents' books. Then she built a replica collection — the same 307 books, the same editions — through entirely legal means. She bought roughly a hundred and fifty titles from bookstores around Los Angeles County. The next hundred or so she found on trips to San Francisco, Seattle, and New York. Everything else she had to order from Berlin, London, and Paris.

Over the course of a year, Julia exchanged one collection for the other, the replica for the original. Every Monday and Wednesday she traveled to the Northridge library with four or five books in a backpack, requested copies of those same books, and switched them when no one was looking. She also transferred the library cards from old to new, possibly because she wanted to cover her tracks, possibly because she was obsessive. It was a victimless crime, and if she hadn't tried to retrieve her parents' other possessions — their jewelry, silverware, and furniture — no one would have been the wiser. In 1975, she was discovered in Mr. Moses Harbaugh's bedroom with a pair of real pearl cuff links and a pair of fake pearl cuff links (she wasn't made of money). Asked by a detective to explain herself, she spilled her guts.

The prosecutor went easy on Julia and the jury took pity, sentencing her to six months of community service. She had to return the jewels and silverware, but the Northridge library said she could keep her parents' books. They were doing just fine with the replacements.

Anna Brisker was a graduate student in English at Collegiate University. She read Frederick Langley's notebooks at the Elston Library and wondered if, by doing so, she had disrespected the author's intentions. In consultation with the author's niece, Anna bought generic marble-cover notebooks and doctored them to look as old as the real things. Leaving them in the sun did most of the work. Anna considered filling them with random text — *lorem ipsum dolor sit amet* — but she didn't know how to disguise her handwriting. Their insides didn't matter anyway. They were meant to serve only as temporary decoys.

On a second trip to the Elston, Anna waited until no one was looking and swapped real for fake. Exactly according to plan, a librarian returned the dummy copies to the stacks without bothering to examine them. Next, Anna delivered the real notebooks to the author's niece for safekeeping. The university suspected what had happened, but could never prove it.

That was one scenario.

A Soft Target

Dr. Lambert covered her mouth to muffle laughter. She was talking — apparently sharing jokes — with a man whose back was turned to me. His blond hair formed a sharp line on his neck, two inches above the brown collar of a forest-green Barbour jacket. Instantly my mood changed from anxious to angry. It was Evan.

"Are we here for the same reason?" I asked, not yet willing to accept the logical deduction.

"Well, yes."

"Carl didn't tell you Evan would be here this time?" asked Dr. Lambert, meaning Professor Davidoff.

After I'd mentioned the notebooks at the cemetery picnic, Evan had, it seemed, approached his adviser, who in turn had approached mine, who, lacking a sense of loyalty or decency, had revealed everything he knew. The library staff figured they weren't really breaking the court-ordered rules if they let a student not approved by Helen Langley (Evan) tag along with a student who was (me), which had led to the present state of affairs.

I felt as though Evan had broken into my house or, more apt, like he'd stolen my boyfriend. I'd skipped down the suburban pathway expecting a romantic tête-à-tête and found Evan sitting shotgun in

Langley's car. Except it was even worse than that, because the boyfriend-stealing floozy was also a potential witness — if a crime occurred, which maybe one would and maybe one would not. The future was foggy with possibility. I felt the weight of the dummy notebooks in my bag.

Dr. Lambert delivered the same old speech about oily fingers and then left us alone, just the three of us: Langley, yours truly, and my once and future rival. Since I'd already had a session with the notebooks, Evan said it was only fair that he would get to read them in chronological order while I would read them in reverse, second first. I stared at Evan as he started in, invading Langley's private space. I could have punched his perfect nose. His nostrils were so small they seemed ornamental. It must have been difficult for him to breathe.

Evan put away his pencil, the universal sign that he was quite finished.

"What a mess," he said in a stage whisper.

"Sorry?"

"I just feel bad for the guy. One notebook's full of half-baked ideas and silly jokes, the other's somehow thin and ponderous at the same time. He was so self-pitying. *Fine,* I kept thinking, *you're angry at your dad! But what was so bad about Dad, really? Dad pushed you to do better by comparing you to your brother — and you found that oppressive? So you try to make a hero out of a guy who makes nothing, no money, nothing of himself? Please.* His stories weren't revolutionary, but at least they were polished and fun. He clearly lost it."

There was no point in telling Evan how wrong he was. It took talent to recognize talent, as someone pithier than I had once said, more or less.

"I guess this trip was a waste of time for you, then."

Evan assumed the position he favored in the classroom: legs crossed, arms crossed, chin up for the camera.

"Not necessarily. I think I can see my way to an article or two, maybe an essay for *Notes and Queries* about Langley's allusive style. The novel's basically his take on *Oblomov*, the Russian novel about extreme laziness. Or I can write something psychoanalytic about how he coped with his evident writer's block — so many years without producing a thing — by making a virtue of failure."

Evan was grinding up Langley in his interpretation machine, but he didn't realize he didn't have the whole picture. He didn't know what he didn't know. Then again, I wondered if an impartial judge presented with both of our arguments would prefer his. It was so much simpler and more direct, the Occam's razor to my Rube Goldberg. I lifted my bag off the floor to once again feel the weight of the dummy notebooks. They were there. They were ready. But I couldn't imagine going through with it.

"What do you think his intentions were?" I asked.

"I just told you."

"For the notebooks, I mean."

"Authors, in my experience, write to be read."

"The first one's so personal, though. And the second — it's all about an artist who can take pleasure only in the work he hides and destroys. 'No I said no I will Not.' Langley saw himself in that artist, in Jonah. You see where I'm going."

"If he'd wanted the notebooks destroyed, he would have destroyed them."

"Except he didn't have time. He died suddenly."

"He didn't *make* the time. You know the story, right? The car accident. Sounds borderline premeditated to me."

"Now, that's a leap!" I countered.

"Hardly. That would fit my portrait of him perfectly. He had writer's block. He ran away to Europe and when he came home he was wrecked, a grown man in an attic, ranking salads in order of personal preference, throwing milk at protesters. Writer's block is difficult for any artist to handle, but especially someone like Langley, whose father was so demanding. Langley was angry at his dad. But his anger, ultimately, was generative. Finally he could write again, about a father's severity and the son's decision to answer the call to do something with the determination to do nothing. That kept him going through a first draft. Then, the adrenaline gone, he thought: *What's the point, writing or not writing?* And he got behind the wheel. He left no will because he didn't care one way or the other."

Everyone seemed to agree that the Elston would win the lawsuit. It would make the notebooks widely available, sell the rights to a commercial publisher. Meanwhile I would try to spin their contents into fodder for my dissertation. And then I would try to sell Professor Davidoff on the idea. And then if he liked it, which given my track record wasn't likely, I would use the dissertation to get a job. And then I would have a job for years and years, years and years of work, until some institution made me a professor emerita, like Barrett Pippen, and I no longer had to research or write or teach or really produce anything at all. Evan would also treat the notebooks as fodder, except that he was further ahead, having already finished his dissertation.

Or I could put to use that heaviness I felt whenever I lifted my bag off the floor.

"I suppose you just gave me a preview of what you'll say in that article or two."

"Yup."

It seemed wrong to build our futures on Langley's back. He'd stopped publishing as a young man in part because he didn't want meddling readers, readers like us, nosing about his work. It was doubtful he'd ever revised that opinion.

"It's so — parasitic."

"What?"

" 'Essay-writers take an author's words and put them to work, turning their potential into kinetic energy.' "

"You're babbling."

"You're a parasite. Eavesdropper. Spy. Voyeur. Peeping Tom. Thief. Vulture. Pick your synonym, because you're going to take this stuff —" A patron at the next table over hushed us; hushed me, rather. In my anger I'd raised my voice. More gently, I went on, "You're going to take Freddy's life, his words, his thoughts, and plunder them for the sake of your career just as soon as the lawsuit's over."

"Freddy? You're on a first-name basis? And what is it that you're doing here if not plundering and thieving just like me?"

As if on cue I heard a loud rumbling and felt the floor shift. *As if on cue:* classic pathetic fallacy. The sound of books falling from shelves preceded gasps from the assembled readers. Pencils rolled off tables. Erasers bounced off the floor. My stomach lurched. I guessed we were experiencing a small earthquake, even though, so far as I knew, there were no fault lines underneath New Harbor.

Someone shouted: "Look!"

We — all of us in the room — left our chairs and approached the glass wall, standing close enough to see the sky beyond the sunken courtyard. We gazed at a dark plume of smoke rising southwest of us. I had a new guess, informed by the times: not an earthquake but a terrorist attack. Yet the media had treated it as such a joke when, after 9/11, Homeland Security had put New Harbor on its list of "soft targets."

"It's just the New Harbor Coliseum," said Evan. He laughed, as did the others standing next to us, staring upward at the smoke. It was the laughter of relief. But I still had no idea what was happening. "The implosion was scheduled for today," he continued.

"An implosion can shake the ground like that?"

"I guess so. NPR had a segment on the coliseum recently. The host said it might be possible to hear the collapse as far away as Meriden."

Wind penetrated the plume of smoke, breaking up the column and spreading dust evenly across the sky. It looked as if it were about to rain. But second by second the darkness dissipated. Cracks of blue revealed themselves in the gray murk, stretched out, widened, reclaiming lost territory. Particles of what had been the New Harbor Coliseum seeped into the atmosphere, contributing infinitesimally to the region's air pollution. Soon the last visual traces of the implosion would disappear.

Since reading the nostalgic feature in the local paper, I hadn't followed any implosion-related news. Although I'd told myself on that occasion that I didn't care what happened to the place, I felt saddened on the reporter's behalf. The location of his first kiss was no more. So much energy had been expended to build the coli-

seum, so much effort, and now it was gone, not through the vindic-
tive violence of an angry terrorist, but through the precise,
organized violence of a government determined to rub out its
mistakes. I did think it was that: A mistake. Yet the people who'd
built it had obviously thought otherwise and would never have
anticipated how short a time their creation would have to lord it
over the city of New Harbor. The sense of impermanence was getting to me.

And then, still watching the sky clear, I reversed myself,
betraying the reporter. Maybe even the New Harbor Coliseum's
architect felt happy, if he were living, that the thing was gone.
Maybe it had been a constant embarrassment to him. Even if he'd
loved it, others had not. Not every idea was worth developing. Not
every developed idea was worth preserving. There was peace in
erasure.

Evan and I walked back to the table where the notebooks lay
waiting, vulnerable and exposed. If I did nothing, Evan would
profit from them. Eventually I would too. We hadn't quite reached
our place when we heard a noise like a smoke detector crossed with
a police siren. Acting on instinct, we covered our ears and molded
our faces into our best *What now?* expressions. A security guard—
the sports fan who'd signed me in the first time—told us to "pro-
ceed calmly" to the exit.

"Jesus," said Evan. "I guess the implosion triggered the alarm."

I raised my voice so Evan could hear me over the din: "Do they
pump the halon gas in here or just into the stacks?"

"I don't really want to find out," he shouted.

Evan did as the security guard advised. I looked around. Evan
wasn't paying attention to me. Neither was the guard nor anyone

else. They all had their backs turned to me as they rushed toward the exit. I looked around again. Evan was already out of sight.

The guard at the main entrance knew he couldn't do his job thoroughly and seemed unsure how to handle the outflow of people. With the alarm still blaring, he glanced inside my backpack. No matter; if I'd hidden the Gutenberg Bible in there, he wouldn't have noticed. Besides, my backpack held no contraband, only the dummy notebooks I'd decided not to leave behind. The library population seeped out of the building and dribbled onto the plaza, moving first as a coherent mass, then disaggregating into individual units. One pixel in forest green caught my eye: Evan. I sneaked past him and headed south.

Just beyond Main Street a beggar blocked my path. He opened his mouth wide and inhaled deeply, like a baby storing up air before a good cry. When his words came, they rushed out in a torrent, reminding me of a wind-up toy: "Please miss please miss spare some change I'm so cold I'm so hungry I'm a veteran please miss anything just a dollar just a nickel just a dime just a penny anything it's so cold I need food I'm not an addict I have no house no car no one will help me will you help me?"

The man repelled and annoyed me. His face was filthy, his pants were torn, and my right arm was sore from flexing. I wanted to get where I was going. But when I pivoted to get around him, the beggar pivoted too, mirroring me in a grotesque dance. Mouth open, springs winding tight: "Please miss I need help I have no one no family I'm hungry I'm cold I need food just a dime."

It seemed, karmically, a little unwise to let down someone so determined. But as I reached for my wallet, the muscles in my right arm, unaccustomed to strenuous activity, contracted. Pain stretched from my rhomboids to my fingertips, and the notebooks tumbled down the inside of my coat onto the sidewalk.

Dr. Lambert had said not to touch the pages too much. She hadn't mentioned anything about dropping the notebooks on dirty concrete. They seemed fine, though. I scooped them up and transferred them to my backpack — a safe move once I'd cleared security, a move that, in my disorder, it hadn't occurred to me to execute earlier. I gave the beggar a dollar and went on my way, grateful to have regained the use of my right arm.

"Thank you miss thank you," the beggar shouted after me.

At each red light I occupied myself by counting until I had the right-of-way. I felt the double weight of the real plus the dummy notebooks in my bag. They knocked against one another. What a lot of trouble I'd gone to for those decoys, a clumsy device obviated by the implosive distraction. The best-laid schemes, et cetera, although in this case they hadn't gone awry, just changed in detail as they became a reality, a reality I hadn't quite believed would ever come about. I'd sensed an opportunity and I'd felt compelled to take the opportunity. Fortune favored the slapdash.

Thinking seemed troublesome. Thinking was inevitable. I thought about my first day on campus, the first time I saw the Elston, the first time I went home for vacation and told an old acquaintance that I was a graduate student at Collegiate. I thought about the day I passed my oral exams. I thought about the grin disappearing from Professor Davidoff's face at the café-bookstore. I thought about the need to find a new case study. I thought about how difficult it would be to find a new case study. I thought about how difficulty sometimes blurred into impossibility. I thought about what Evan had said. I thought about the look on Ian's face before he told me about the *Town and Country* article. I thought about that day at the supermarket when Helen asked me to pay her bill. I thought about her swiping her uncle's hardcovers from her father's library. I turned onto St. John Street.

Idiocy and Confusion

The next day I heard nothing from Helen. Although we'd never been in daily contact, this irked me, as it would irk a young woman if the boy she'd been flirting with for months and finally taken to bed failed to call her the morning after. Our relationship had led up — had built up inexorably — to the night before and we'd had such a boisterous and intimate evening. She'd been so pleased with me.

Nor did Helen call on the second day, nor on the third. Silence led to anxiety led to suspicion. Suspicion that since she now possessed what she had long wanted, she would have no further use for me. Could it be that she'd never cared for me except as an instrument? But on the fourth day I realized there was no reason for me to assume that contact was Helen's responsibility. Unlike the young woman and the boy, there was no social etiquette dictating that Helen had to make the first or, rather, post-facto move. *I'm just calling to say I had a lovely time. Thank you so much for the stolen goods.* It occurred to me that Helen was quite possibly wondering why I hadn't called, that she was going through the same mental contortions as I. On day five, I resolved to wait one more day.

On day six, Professor Davidoff dropped by unannounced. He must have asked the English department secretary for my address. Perhaps he'd made up some excuse as to why he needed it, or perhaps not. The secretary had never liked me.

Helen had warned me — that boisterous evening — that this might happen. Her advice in mind, I affected what I considered the adequate amount of surprise and invited my adviser inside. I said I'd make coffee. From the kitchen I could hear him creeping around the sitting room, lifting things up and putting them back down.

"Your apartment is unexpectedly nice, Anna," he said when I delivered his mug.

We sat across from each other on identical Le Corbusier couches, my glass table between us. I feigned deep absorption in my coffee before asking, as if just by the way: "What is it you wanted to talk about?"

"I was wondering," said Professor Davidoff, "what you thought of Frederick Langley's notebooks. You've been to see them twice now but you haven't said a word."

"Sorry, it hadn't occurred to me. That was rude. Actually, I think they're fascinating. Messy, not meant for an audience, but fascinating."

We added cream and sugar to our coffees. We sipped our coffees. The professor had a prominent blood vessel running down the center of his forehead that pulsed when he was frustrated. It pulsed now. I smiled in return, trying my best to look like a pleasant idiot. *Evelyn*, I thought. *I should try to look like Evelyn: vacant expression, lips open a smidgen to reveal a few front teeth.*

"Do you see any potential for your dissertation?"

"Possibly," I said, holding my chin. "They support my theory for why Langley stopped writing and why he started again — his de- and re-inspiration, more or less. But in order to advance it, I'd also have to argue that even reading the notebooks is a violation of Langley's desire for privacy."

"Anna, do you remember what you did with the notebooks before you left the library?"

His voice cracked and the vessel pulsed.

"Not really. Nothing, I think." I paused to suggest spontaneous thought in progress. "I know I was supposed to put them back in the metal container and return them to the security guard, but that didn't seem like a priority when the implosion triggered the alarm. You heard all about that, I'm sure. I thought at first we were experiencing an earthquake... Why? Were they damaged?"

"Something like that."

"I guess that explains your visit. I'm sorry. I followed Dr. Lambert's care instructions — not touching the pages too much or folding them over. Did you realize Evan was there too? I can't vouch for him. And anyone could have handled them after the alarm."

"Do you have anything to tell me?"

"Like what?"

"Mind if I look around?" he asked.

He was struggling to sound casual, but his voice was hardening, turning to anger, whereas my expression conveyed idiocy and confusion. Or so I hoped. Really, I wanted to laugh. If the library staff suspected me, which apparently they did, why send an English professor to play detective? Even assuming I'd kept the notebooks in my apartment, how could Professor Davidoff expect to turn them up by just "looking around," unless I'd hidden them some-where obvious, like under the couch, or left them in plain sight? The Elston staff must have been eager to keep the notebooks' dis-appearance quiet. Instead of contacting the police, they had depu-tized Professor Davidoff, who at that moment was parting my window curtains to inspect the sills. They must have believed that his mere presence would make me want to talk.

"I could give you a tour, if you want, but there's not much to see and I didn't make my bed this morning."

"That's not what I meant," said Professor Davidoff. "If I were to, say, check underneath this couch, would I find anything? What if I opened your freezer or your kitchen cabinets?"

"If you're lucky you'll find some Pop-Tarts," I said, smiling vapidly. I remained seated with my legs crossed while the professor paced. "Clearly you're implying something, but I really don't know what. Maybe Evan—"

"Forget Evan," Professor Davidoff said sharply. "Anna, I know. I know what you did, but I don't know why. When Kristen told me what happened, I only suspected you a little. Neither of us believed it could be Evan. He wouldn't risk his career. But then I talked to Ian Jackson. Do you know who that is?"

"No."

"Yes, you do."

"Don't think so."

"Think harder."

"Drawing a blank."

"You visited his house in Milford."

Helen's cousin Ian had not shared his last name. I had answered truthfully and yet technically I had just lied, so the professor would assume my intention was deceit, which made me nervous. Strange that an accidental lie made me feel queasy whereas straightforward falsehood came naturally enough.

"Oh, right. That Ian."

"He called the department a while ago. He said a young woman named Anna Brisker interrupted him one afternoon when he was gardening, claimed she was a graduate student studying Frederick Langley, and asked to see the house for research. Ian told me he took all this in stride but decided to get in touch after noticing that this young woman had rifled through the boxes in his attic."

"So what?"

"So that's odd behavior, don't you think? Even for a socially odd person like you? I didn't think much about the call at first and, under normal circumstances, would have promptly forgotten it. But, frankly, these aren't normal circumstances."

"You still haven't explained why — haven't said what's abnormal."

Look like Evelyn. Look like Evelyn. Vacant expression. Open lips. No, closed. Evelyn's canines were whiter than mine.

"Ian was worried for another reason," the professor continued, ignoring my insincerity. He loomed above me with that pulsing vessel. "You told him you knew his cousin."

I grunted.

"That woman is an enemy of this university. She's been after those notebooks for years. Do you know how valuable they are? The notebooks of a famous author? Any publishing house would pay a fortune for the rights."

"Come on. Everyone's so dismissive of Langley. You were dismissive when I first mentioned him."

"There's a difference between worthy of study and popular. Every bookish kid in America has read one or two of his stories. Even on the black market, his notebooks would fetch mid–six figures, at least. The judge should have dismissed her case a long time ago."

The professor seemed on the brink of enjoying himself. In his daily life he would rarely have had occasion to call someone an enemy. Although he wanted to sound serious, like a political leader in a time of war, he reminded me of a middle-school girl sparring with her chief rival for some lug-head's attention.

"She's a crook," he said. "Her parents disowned her because she kept stealing from them. It's sickening. She even stole their first edition of *Alone at Green Beach* and tried to sell it to the Elston — long before the lawsuit."

"Where'd you hear that?" I allowed myself to ask.

"Kristen told me."

It seemed unwise for me to suggest that I knew more of Helen's story than my adviser did and that, in context, her behavior wasn't too bad. Anyway, Helen's crooked past meant little to me when weighed against the fact that, in the present, she was carrying out Freddy Langley's will. Professor Davidoff continued pacing.

"You befriend this woman, a thief chasing our notebooks. Suddenly you decide you want to study Langley. Suddenly you show up at a stranger's house, go through his belongings. You make an appointment at the library to read the notebooks, then another, and, suddenly, that same day, the notebooks vanish."

"What? They're gone?" I flung my hands in the air to indicate shocked distress. If I'd left behind the dummy notebooks, as originally planned, there would have been no room for me to maneuver;

their presence would have been proof of intentional absence. For-tunately, the implosion had changed my strategy. "Maybe they're just lying around somewhere in the library. Maybe they were mis-placed in the mayhem?"

"You're not a good actress, frankly. And this is a serious crime."

"I have absolutely no idea what you're talking about, but I'm starting to think I should get a lawyer."

It was an alarming word in certain circumstances. The Elston didn't want another lawsuit, let alone a criminal investigation that would jeopardize its chances of winning the first lawsuit. Only a poor steward would let such valuable items vanish, and a poor steward didn't deserve custody. The professor scratched the dry skin around his nose, indicating that his anger was reconfiguring itself and would soon settle into anxiety. He scratched and paced and sighed.

"I'll leave now," he said. "But I'm sure even you are perceptive enough to realize that I can't be your adviser anymore."

Pure Pointlessness

I was a seventh-year graduate student in New Harbor and then I was a former graduate student in New Harbor. On a résumé, the difference was everything. Second to second, the two states were identical. Looking in the mirror after Professor Davidoff left, telling myself it was really over, all over, I noticed no change in my appearance. I coiled a gray hair around my index finger and extracted it from my scalp. *You'll look better once you've had a little sun.* I leaned forward, pressed my temple against the cold glass. That vantage point revealed a grimy palimpsest: layer upon layer of fingerprints. Some were whole, a detective's fantasy, others smudged beyond the recognition of the best forensic scientists.

Of course, it was all over before the professor's visit. It was all over when I took the notebooks. Or maybe it was all over years ago. But not until he came and left was the truth undeniable. Until he left, I could tell myself that I could move on to another case study. How hard could that be? Not that I truly believed that little story, but until recently I could tell it — if only to myself. Now I couldn't anymore.

My appearance hadn't changed. My behavior probably wouldn't change much either. Before the professor's visit I wasn't making any progress on my dissertation. After the professor's visit, I wouldn't make any progress on my dissertation. Stasis was stasis. Silence was silence. The pointlessness of my New Harbor existence, once a dereliction of duty, was finally pure. I did nothing and now I wasn't supposed to do anything. Judging from the mirror, I was grinning like a maniac. I could feel it, too, my cheeks rising up so high my eyes narrowed.

I wanted to share these thoughts with Helen. I could confide in no one else. She didn't return my phone calls, though — *calls*, plural, more than two, less than four — and when I went by her house, she didn't answer the door. Guessing without evidence that she'd return sooner rather than later, I resolved to wander before checking in again.

Eventually, I would have to tell my parents. Before that, I would need a plan. Or, alternatively, a plan for how to tell my parents that I didn't want a plan? There was something so morbid about having a career, staying on a track, something so limiting and inhumane about self-improvement and advancement, wasn't there? There was nothing wrong with nothing, for a while, at least, was there? What if I did nothing? I would bide my time. Read without underlining or taking notes. Walk around. Eat. Sleep. Maybe keep a notebook.

Mom and Dad, I would say, or I could imagine myself saying. *Uncle Joshua was meant to be a doctor and you thought I was meant to study literature — I thought so too — but as it turns out, I wasn't. Maybe I was meant to do nothing.*

Nothing?

Nothing.

You're lazy. You have to maximize your potential.

I plan to maximize my laziness.

If it was a pose, it was as good as any other. I could try it on and see how I liked it.[5]

---

5   *A phone conversation between Anna and her family's banker, Harry.*
HARRY: You're kidding me, seven years?
ANNA: No, six and a half.
HARRY: Rounding up's not against the law. It'll be seven years soon. When do you finish?
ANNA: I keep trying to tell you. There's a delay.
HARRY: Seven years?
ANNA: Must you keep repeating that?
HARRY: Sorry.
ANNA: I need to plan for the future. That's why I called.
HARRY: One point five.
ANNA: That's good, one point five.
HARRY: I'll say.
ANNA: What's that do in a year?
HARRY: It depends.
ANNA: On what?
HARRY: On a lot of things. Mainly the market.
ANNA: Let's assume the market does not great and not terrible, just fine.
HARRY: You have to understand this is just speculation.
ANNA: Yeah.
HARRY: Could you answer in a complete sentence so I can say you understood if you sue me?
ANNA: I understand that you're just speculating.
HARRY: The way it's invested so far, about sixty.
ANNA: A year?
HARRY: A year. In perpetuity.
ANNA: That's not much.
HARRY: Plus your stipend and what your parents chip in, that's been enough. Whatever comes next, you'll make more than now, don't you think? What do junior professors make? Like, ninety?
ANNA: I keep telling you, I might not get there.

Professor Davidoff had dismissed me from his life and, in a way, from my life. A listless future stretched out before me, and it seemed glorious. When I thought about stealing the notebooks, I felt no regret. I felt rocked by prideful pleasure. I'd taken my chance. I'd moved quickly. I'd hidden the notebooks under my coat, right above my hips, at loin level, and with my right arm kept them pressed against my torso. Visualizing that moment made me lose control of my facial capillaries. I mean it made me blush. The coliseum imploded. The sky absorbed the smoke. I walked back to my table. The alarm sounded. I saw the notebooks. I took them, leaving the dummies in my bag. I blushed. The alarm sounded. Evan turned his back. No witnesses. I took the notebooks. I blushed. I took the notebooks.

In a counterfactual history of my twenties that climaxed with me turning in a dissertation, how would my sense of pride and sat-

---

HARRY: You mean *ever?* Anna, you're not thinking you'll just have the sixty?

ANNA: I keep telling you—

HARRY: Would your parents help like they do now?

ANNA: Doubt it.

HARRY: You'd have to keep an eye on expenses. Make a budget. Keep a budget.

ANNA: What about the principal?

HARRY: You know how that works. Dip in one year, you don't get sixty the next.

ANNA: Do the math for me. Dip in to get me to seventy-five—no, ninety, same as a junior professor after a raise or two. No, I don't want to live like a professor. Double that, to one-eighty. How long?

HARRY: It depends.

ANNA: I understand you're just speculating.

HARRY: Twelve, thirteen years.

ANNA: Not bad!

HARRY: Twice the amount of time you've spent in New Harbor.

isfaction compare? Would I blush each time I thought about printing out my thesis for the last time, then getting it bound? Maybe not. Probably not. For years I'd dedicated myself to figuring out what authors were trying to say and then writing about it in a near vacuum (only one person, a professor, would read my work). At the Elston I'd figured out what an author, Langley, wanted to say, or how he felt, and I'd actually done something about it — something concrete. And that something was useful — to the author. Not to mention to his niece, my friend.

I imagined the notebooks as they had been, in the Elston stacks, in a metal container, and as they were now: safe at Helen's. I pictured them in Helen's bedroom, in her bottom dresser drawer, where she kept the *Qui transtulit sustinet* postcard; in a closet; in a kitchen cabinet; in the study next to *Gone with the Wind* and the unpaid bills; buried in her backyard. Except it was made out of concrete. Buried in the New Harbor Green, then. When I'd suggested to Helen that we bury the notebooks, like burying talent in the ground, she'd smiled. She'd found that a little too cute. Screw Professor Davidoff. Screw the Elston. I had done right by Langley and right by his niece, finally restoring the notebooks to her keeping.

My moral righteousness had come at a cost. The cost was my career. Its value was hard to establish, debatably close to zero. But I had money enough for an alternative, for a while. One-eighty a year for twelve or thirteen years. Why not? The life of a professor emerita. The life — so said the sandwich wrapper — of the Mexican fisherman.

I circled up to First Campus and came upon a lathy boy showing his parents around. "That's a statue of Paul Revere," the boy told his mother and father, "the Revolutionary War hero who never said, 'The British are coming.' He said: 'The Regulars are coming out.' Come on! We're going to be late!"

He was keenly aware that the people who had brought him into the world and brought him up were finally on his turf. Accordingly, he played at tour guide and then, cruelly, rolled his eyes when his parents stopped to take pictures or asked for more information. He was drunk with control.

"Come on!" he whined.

I followed the trio, lagging far enough behind so they wouldn't notice me but close enough to overhear their conversation. They walked slowly, luxuriating in the first not-cold, almost-warm day of mid-March. Did they realize the unpleasant days would come back, killing off the flower buds naive enough to think it was spring in earnest? New Harbor was a subtle beast, weather-wise, subtly lethal.

Mom asked the boy if he was dating anyone. He sneered and looked away, asserting his right to privacy and independence. But he must have wanted desperately to confide in someone, because as soon as Mom apologized for asking, he shared his story.

Noah, the lathy boy, had met Olivia before classes started, on a five-night hiking trip for rising freshmen. He liked her right away. She was sporty and direct. She wore her hair pulled back in a ponytail but did not chemically straighten it to fit white beauty standards; she had no need for makeup. She was exactly his type. On the second night, the seniors leading the hike asked for volunteers to gather dry wood for a fire. Olivia volunteered, so Noah did too.

They'd traveled a fair distance when Olivia's flashlight went dark and the warm, late-summer breeze instantly turned cold. Leaves rustled angrily. Owls hooted fiercely. A cloud passed over the moon. Noah and Olivia stopped, as they say, dead in their tracks. And not ten steps ahead a man materialized. He was extraordinarily tall! He was extraordinarily pale! He was holding a hatchet! Olivia dropped the wood they'd gathered so meticulously, turned, and ran. Noah followed. Finally, back in sight of camp and comforting company, Olivia caught her breath and asked Noah what, oh my God, what they should tell the others.

"That we got spooked by a hiker, I guess," he said.

"That's probably best," said Olivia cryptically.

It turned out Olivia was 100 percent certain that they'd encountered a ghost. No human being was that tall or that pale. No *living* human being. The ghost's presence had interfered with the flashlight and summoned the cold wind. What was he holding in his hand? The other hand, not the one with the hatchet? Olivia had thought at first that it was a dead animal. Perhaps, though, it was a dead baby. Noah didn't believe a word of this, but eighteen-year-olds with crushes aren't always the most honest creatures.

"You're so right," Noah said. "It was probably a dead baby."

On this foundation, Noah and Olivia built a relationship. Noah was so happy to have a girlfriend that he didn't care that she was crazy. He bought her a Ouija board and suggested they try to make contact with Hatchet Man, as they called him, by candlelight. B-a-b-y, said the board, confirming Olivia's suspicions. H-o-r-r-i-b-l-e-c-r-i-m-e. They read *The Malleus Maleficarum* aloud and had earnest conversations about the afterlife. College was grand.

But then, a few weeks prior to his parents' visit, disaster. Noah and Olivia went to a party at one of the fraternities. A hockey player with preposterously broad shoulders took notice of Olivia and began flirting with her while Noah hung back, trying not to seem wounded. He was a big, brutally good-looking guy, the hockey player, but girls didn't care for such specimens after graduating from high school, did they? As was fairly typical for her, Olivia spouted some nonsense about ghosts, and the hockey player laughed in her face. Noah thought Olivia would take offense. Instead she laughed back.

"I guess I sounded pretty dumb just now," she said.

In short order Olivia forgot about Hatchet Man and she forgot about Noah, too, throwing both men over for the hockey player and a more rational life.

"I thought I was giving her what she wanted," Noah told his mom and dad.

"It's always hard to know what a woman really wants, son," said Dad. "And that's true even when she's told you what she wants."

The sorry bunch went north and I south, back to Worcester Square. I passed several couples on the way and asked myself if they were more like Noah and Olivia or Olivia and the hockey player. In his weakness, Noah had reflected Olivia's folly. He'd thought he'd be safe so long as he was a mirror. In his strength, the hockey player realized that apparent convictions were rarely deep — convictions were often no more than fads. The boy in the red sweatshirt was a hockey player. The boy in the navy peacoat was a Noah.

By the time I got back to Helen's street, it was dark out and her lights were on. She must have returned while I was following Noah. But when I rang her bell she didn't come to the door. I waited a few minutes, walked around Worcester Square Park, came back — and found the lights were off. So she'd left the house with the lights on, come home, turned them off? This was odd. Or had she gone to sleep already? It wasn't yet eight p.m. I rang the bell. Nothing again. I trudged down the front steps, went over to her study window, and pressed my face against the glass as I'd pressed my face against the mirror earlier that day. Once my eyes adjusted a bit I realized I was staring right at Helen. We must have become aware of each other at exactly the same moment. She recovered from the shock and pointed left, toward the front door.

"What are you doing here?" she asked brusquely, over the threshold.

"Why didn't you answer?" I asked simultaneously.

Clumsily we established that I should go first.

"I haven't seen you since last week, since — and I wanted to check in. To talk to you. To tell you about—"

"You shouldn't have come. What if someone sees us together?"

"You think someone followed me here?"

"I'm not crazy, just cautious. The safe thing is for you to keep your distance."

"Will you at least tell me where you're keeping them? I'm curious."

"You should go."

"Let me in, just for a few minutes."

"Maybe if I didn't have a guest."

"A guest?"

"A man."

"A man?"

"You should go."

It was a strange thing to find myself in such a movie. Professor

Carl Davidoff as the cunning sleuth and Helen Langley, antiquarian, as the sober co-conspirator worried that her young partner lacked the constitution for secrecy. I'd stolen the notebooks in the course of things, as the natural offshoot of my ordinary life. But the other characters wanted to enforce a break between before and after.

I hurried home in a fit of adolescent rage, which was to say depression, walking briskly past anyone who seemed to notice my distress. I told myself Helen would call me when the man left. I told myself that, if I fell ill again, she'd hurry to my side. I wondered if the day's tumult would, in fact, make me ill again. I remembered reading "Alone at Green Beach" for the first time, the sense of frustration and desolate disappointment triggered by another memory.

When I turned twelve my mother decided I was old enough to fast on Yom Kippur, the Jewish Day of Atonement. She would fast as well. Although we were too secular to bother with synagogue, we—or she, rather—felt it was important to connect on a metaphysical-cultural level with the other members of our tribe. Hence the deprivation. To avoid thoughts of food we went to the nearby natural history museum. The elaborate dioramas and the taxidermy statues were absorbing enough that I forgot my more primal needs. I barely even noticed, upon leaving the museum, the scent of hot dogs and pretzels and roasted nuts from the street vendors who always gathered by the exit.

But my mother said, "Do you want a little something? It must be tempting."

"I'm not supposed to," I said.

"If you can't get through the day, no one will blame you."

"It's not much longer. I can do it."

"You're just a little girl."

And then I did smell the hot dogs and pretzels and roasted nuts. And then desire won its battle with abstemious pride. My mother bought me a salted pretzel with mustard. To keep me company, as she said, she bought herself the same. We agreed not to reveal our transgression to my father. But when we got back home, he noticed a yellow stain on my blouse.

"I think I know what that is," he said. "And I don't think the sun has set."

My mother, annoyed, stern: "Don't shame her. When she told me she was hungry, what could I do? You would have done the same thing."

The incident was so silly and base, it seemed absurd to claim it as an injury. Even a gentle psychotherapist would have chuckled at my expense before urging me to forget the parable of the mustard stain. In that particular farce, unlike in Freddy's story, there was no epiphanic closure. There was no catharsis.

A Letter of Explanation

Miss Anna Brisker
The Roosevelt, Apartment 2D
New Harbor, Connecticut

Dear Miss Brisker,

Despite your paranoid concerns, the receptionist passed along
your letter unopened. What a lot of questions. Starting with your
obsession with my use of the word "funny." In a word, I find it
funny, as in perplexing. I think you're spinning mysteries where
there are none. "Funny" means "funny," as in "silly." You could
have just come out and asked directly why Freddy Langley
stopped writing. For goodness sake, I was his editor and I know
the answer. He didn't feel like writing anymore, didn't see the
point. That's all. End of story. Finis. When he lived in Europe I
asked him to send me pages and he said he didn't have any.

I know all about the notebooks too and I can tell you that your
precious "look after" line is a lot of nonsense. Freddy never asked
his niece to look after the notebooks. He couldn't have because he
wanted me to edit them for him. Well, the second one, the one he
wrote after his father died, the one he told me about the last time I

saw him. That was at his father's funeral. Freddy said he planned to write a "letter of explanation" in novel form. He had in mind some kind of meta project on his characters' motives, I believe. When I asked him if it had commercial potential, he didn't say no, which was his way of saying yes. He certainly never approached another editor so that leaves yours truly,

Richard Anders

P.S. If he'd wanted his niece to "look after" his work, he would have made a will before getting in the car. You must have heard all of this by now. Six or seven months after his father's funeral he drove to the cemetery. From there, he went to a bar and had far too many drinks. It began to rain. He rushed out when the roads were at their most slippery, before the oil and dust had washed away. The bartender should have stopped him. Freddy knew what he was doing.

Of Course

A blueberry Pop-Tart leaped out of the toaster. Its sibling stayed behind, trapped under the metal opening. Disobeying childhood lessons, I stuck a fork in the slot to spring it loose. Then I poured myself a glass of milk, less because I wanted one than to occupy myself while the pastries cooled. Even so, I burned my tongue on synthetic goo. The day was ruined. The only reasonable thing to do was return to bed and, to counteract the slothfulness of daylight horizontality, read the *New York Times* on my laptop.

I would of course have found out eventually. In the moment it was jarring. For a while I lingered on other articles. The tech gurus predicting the success of Apple's revolutionary smartphone months before anyone could buy one; the pundits predicting a Hillary Clinton win in Iowa months before anyone could cast a ballot; in the Styles section, a profile of the disgustingly young entrepreneur behind Mario IRL, a jungle gym for adults with obstacle courses based on Super Mario Brothers. He — the entrepreneur — thought twenty-somethings would pay a premium to jump through large plastic pipes in janitor outfits. Perhaps he was right. At least Mario IRL was flashier than the entrepreneur's first business, a combined car wash and animal clinic. Have a vet check your pet while you get an oil change. Cats and dogs only, please.

When I turned over on my side and clicked back to that distressing article, the facts were the same. Of course they were. The FBI's art-theft unit had been tracking the Danish shipping magnate for years. He was suspected of buying black-market paintings and commissioning spectacular robberies. Some believed he'd actually organized the largest art heist in history—the theft of thirteen paintings from the Isabella Stewart Gardner Museum on March 18, 1990. Finally they'd accumulated enough evidence to search his American pied-à-terre near Santa Fe.

They did not find Vermeer's *The Concert*, Rembrandt's *The Storm on the Sea of Galilee,* or any of the other Gardner-owned paintings. Nor did they find Jan van Eyck's *The Righteous Judges,* missing since April 10, 1934, rumored to have been stolen by the shipping magnate's father. (Theft ran in the family.) But they did turn up an object that no one had even reported lost: A marble notebook that had once belonged to the author Frederick Langley. It contained diary-like material as well as story ideas and was supposed to be sitting safely in Collegiate University's rare-books library, the Elston.

When pressed for information, the Elston acknowledged that the notebook in question, and a companion notebook containing the draft of a novel, had gone missing some weeks before. Convinced the notebooks had simply been misplaced—they'd vanished on the day a nearby explosion had triggered an alarm, and then mayhem, at the library—the staff had not bothered to alert police. (If the reporter confused implosion and explosion, what else had he gotten wrong? Cold comfort, that.)

Although this sounded innocent enough, the report made it obvious that the library had actually committed a significant infraction in keeping the disappearance quiet. Perhaps telling the police was not quite necessary, but administrators should at least have informed Helen Langley, Frederick Langley's niece, currently embroiled in a lawsuit with the Elston over ownership of the notebooks. The Elston had not contacted Ms. Langley at all until after the reporter had started asking questions.

Ms. Langley, the author's sole surviving blood relative, said the library was guilty of negligence and thus had given up the right, if it had ever really had it, to care for the notebooks. (It sounded like she was talking about a child.) On that basis, Ms. Langley argued that a judge should order the police to give her, rather than the Elston, possession of the first notebook, and of the second as well, if it should ever surface. Still unknown was how, exactly, the two notebooks had been stolen, how the shipping magnate had come to have the first—he wasn't talking to the press—and the fate of the second.

Too hot. It was too hot under the down comforter. With just the sheet, though, I was too cold, a classic April dilemma. The solution was to turn up the heat. Or to put on a sweater. More heat plus sheet or sweater plus sheet ought to do it. Either solution would require getting out of bed, though. The comforter was O.K., really, not too bad at all. I could live with it. It was *O,* period, *K,* period. Sure, the groceries and the unpaid bills and her landlord's eviction threats (she needed money), and cousin Ian and *Gone with the Wind* (she'd been a crook, was still a crook), and possibly also rifling through my desk drawers (untrustworthy). But our relationship, and her relationship to her uncle. She'd betrayed him.

I'd taken my chance. I'd moved quickly. I'd hidden the notebooks under my coat, right above my hips, and with my right arm kept them pressed against my torso. The coliseum imploded. The sky absorbed the smoke. I walked back to my table. The alarm sounded. I saw the notebooks. I took them. The alarm sounded. Evan turned his back. No witnesses. I took the notebooks. The only thing I had ever really done for an author, or at all? Something, with the thought of nothing in return.

I thought about Alfred Watt, the Langley character from the first notebook: he got away with a crime and then turned himself in because he wanted recognition. To say I'd gotten away with anything wasn't quite right. The library had been well aware of my guilt from the start. Yet it was impotent in its awareness. Strange that as the situation unraveled and *the tabs took note*, my involvement receded. That is to say, I felt more recognized when as far as the public knew there had been no crime than when the crime was official. Now I seemed to have nothing to do with it at all. I kicked off the comforter. I pushed myself out of bed. I turned up the heat. I went back to bed.

Probably she would win the right to both notebooks in the wake of the perceived lapse. So publicly she would have the first and privately she would have both. Unless she'd already sold the second too. No reason to think that, though. She could give the first back to the Danish shipping magnate or pay him off and sell the first quite openly, at Christie's, say. Or she could keep it while selling the rights to a publisher. The notebooks — considered as pure objects — were more valuable pre-publication, pre-*Frederick Langley's Notebooks,* than post-, because prior to mass production they were the only way to access Langley's thoughts. For the time being his ideas were exclusive to the sheets of paper where he'd happened to record them. Still, while publication would bring down the value of the notebooks as objects, a contract plus royalties would add up to more than whatever a Christie's auction would yield.

But what was I thinking? She could get a contract plus royalties and still sell the notebook itself (for less than if she hadn't signed a contract, fine). So publication plus auction was the most lucrative route, and therefore the most likely one. At least for the first notebook. As for the second, she could essentially launder it — have it turn up somewhere and then sell it at auction and/or sell the rights. Unless she'd already sold it. No reason, though, to think she'd sold it. It was still in her house, I felt certain. In her bedroom, in her bottom dresser drawer, where she kept the *Qui transtulit sustinet* postcard, in a closet, in the study next to *Gone with the Wind*.

It shouldn't have mattered to me. It never had anything to do with me. Though I'd involved myself. I'd done my part, and she'd nullified it. It was over. There was nothing I could do. Mid–six figures at least, Professor Davidoff had said.

Twelve or thirteen years, Harry had said. My grandfather had suffered a stroke, then another, then another. At the end, everyone said it was for the best. We'd gathered around his bed like in an old novel. We'd watched him breathe. He was lucky, everyone said.

Not in the hospital. At home. Surrounded by family. Everyone seemed more relieved than sad. An old man. An old man with money. The physical inheritance came right away: the mahogany desk for a budding scholar. The liquid funds came later. One-eighty for twelve or thirteen years. Principal plus interest for the sake of nothing. Interest for my interest in nothing. Interest and interest. Talent and talent.

The twelve or thirteen years felt hard won. They were anything but. If I gave up a quarter, did that mean nine or ten years? Was that how it worked? If I gave up half, six and a half years? Either way, eventually I'd have to go from nothing to something. Twelve or thirteen wasn't indefinite; it was twelve or thirteen. What did it matter, twelve or thirteen or six and a half? Somehow six and a half seemed far less than half of twelve or thirteen. After three years, which was nothing, less than half the time I'd lived in New Harbor, I would have just three to go, less than half the time I'd lived in New Harbor.

I didn't look like a dupe, did I? I hadn't done all that just for her, had I? Done all that for nothing? For the sake of nothing, but not for nothing. Having done it, it seemed absurd to let it amount to nothing. It was the principle of the thing. The principal.

Would I get up, get dressed, shower, call Harry? Would I start the process? Somehow get it all in cash. Large bills. Go to her house with the cash, in a briefcase or something. A black briefcase. A black leather briefcase with gold-plated locks. She wouldn't be able to resist all that cash right in front of her for the taking. What's not in *Middlemarch*? What didn't she have that I had and so didn't know it mattered? She lacked it and needed it and I barely noticed. To me, it was just a footnote. Would I offer her half the money?

No. Start with a quarter and then go up if necessary? Half and then go up if necessary, so as not to put her off? Twelve or thirteen years, or six and a half years? Get up, and then shower, and then get dressed, and then call the banker, and then walk to Worcester Square, and then six and a half years?

Anna Remembered

Carl Davidoff: At first she was a terrific student, the best in her year. After oral exams, though, when it came time to write a dissertation, she lost it. That's not unusual. Such things happen. There's a big difference between reading books and saying what you think about them on the one hand, and having to produce a dissertation, a major work of scholarship, on the other.

She spent years researching inspiration for her dissertation. She was allergic to the idea that there was anything special about artists and decided that the only key to producing art was work, hard work. She said this was obvious. But for someone so theoretically enamored of discipline, she wasn't disciplined. Like I said, she spent years on her dissertation, but she had trouble finishing and I suspected — knew — that she was good at finding excuses not to sit in front of her computer. She procrastinated. I'm not saying that was her only problem. Certainly it was one problem.

When Anna read about Langley — about how he'd stopped publishing as a young man, then started again — she decided he worked nicely as a case study for her dissertation: He'd been inspired, de-inspired, re-inspired. I don't think she understood her nonprofessional attraction to him, that she saw herself in him because he, like her, was prolific before he was the opposite. But my PhD isn't in psychology.

Anyway, she dismissed the most direct explanation for his silence, plain old writer's block, and invented this ridiculous theory: that Langley hated critics and criticism and, what's more, hated his status as an author. So he became opposed to publishing on philosophical grounds.

This led Anna to assume he wouldn't have wanted his notebooks made public. Take a look at her yellow legal pad, which we were able to confiscate. All the lines she copied from Langley's notebooks were about not sharing one's accomplishments or withholding from the world. It's like she was building a case. All evidence to the contrary, she just ignored. (By the way, it's too bad she didn't transcribe anything from the second notebook because that would have been useful in trying to reconstruct it.)

Convenient, don't you think? She decided it was wrong to produce scholarship based on the notebooks — an open-and-shut preemptive excuse for not being able to produce scholarship based on the notebooks. That's why she took them, or why she told herself she took them, or how she justified taking them. That was her motive, and not the money she must have inveigled in exchange for the notebooks. The money was just a perk. She couldn't very well keep the notebooks around her apartment. So she figured, *Why not?* Obviously we haven't been able to prove any of this but that's what I think.

Evan Edwards: I didn't like her much, honestly, but my fiancée, Evelyn, felt sorry for her, so we'd see her every once in a while. She never had a boyfriend or anything like that. Because Evelyn and I were happy, she'd lash out at us. She'd drop these nasty comments that she thought were really cutting but actually just made her seem pathetic.

Since, like I said, Evelyn felt sorry for her, we invited her to have a picnic with us in the cemetery a few weeks before the incident. I don't remember much about it except she said she couldn't read purely for pleasure anymore — join the club — but did enjoy chasing after authors, metaphorically. Actually, this I remember clearly: She compared figuring something out in literature to hunting down an author, cooking, and eating him. It was odd. And graphic.

The day of the incident, at the library, she seemed like a completely different person. She'd decided academics weren't heroic hunters but eavesdropping parasites. I wasn't totally sure what she was getting at, but I guess she thought, for some reason, that Langley wouldn't have wanted people like us, scholars, to pry.

She kept getting angry, raising her voice. Other people in the library noticed and shushed her. Because I left the library quickly after the alarm went off, I didn't see anything. What everyone says, though, makes sense. She seemed on edge.

Helen Langley: She was a strange young woman. Well, she still is, for all I know, but I haven't seen her in a while. I first met her at a grocery store. I'd forgotten my wallet. She was next to me in line and offered to pay my bill. That was sweet of her, I'll admit. Then a couple of weeks later she saw me on the street and followed me home, knocked on my door to ask for repayment. I was shocked. In itself this was shockingly rude but this wasn't just any day — this was December twenty-fifth! She told me later she hadn't realized. I know she's Jewish but, really, how could someone not realize it was Christmas?

We got to talking. When I learned that she was a graduate student in English at the university, I told her about my uncle. A week or two later she came back to ask questions about him, and I explained the situation with the notebooks. She became completely obsessed with my uncle and those notebooks.

I'm sure she took them. Both of them. I don't know why but who else could have? Maybe she needed the money. I think she still has the other one, the second one—that she kept it. I can't prove it and I'm not saying the police should go looking for it. That's just what I would guess happened, knowing what I know.

Acknowledgments

Thanks above all to Eva, Henry, and Adrienne Lapidos. They shaped my personality, so don't blame me, blame them. Thanks also to the MPO; the Rosenblums; my teachers, especially the ones who cared enough to criticize my writing; my agent, Chris Clemans, the ideal reader; my meticulous editors, Carina Guiterman and Charlotte Cray; the whole Little, Brown staff; and the unsuspecting people whose jokes I lifted in some form (Richard Brodhead and Dermot Dix).

Maria Bustillos was kind enough to read an early version of the manuscript and pretend she liked it. My childhood friends/life partners/death pacters did not read early versions but seem to have forgiven me. Barry Harbaugh not only defended my solitude but also listened patiently when I ranted, complained, or felt sorry for myself. "What's Not in *Middlemarch*" is the title of an article by the British literary critic Dame Gillian Beer. The book *Writer's Block* by Zachary Leader was an indispensable source. Readers familiar with New Haven and its history may wonder, *Haven't I seen this somewhere before?* Yes, you have.